MEGAN

Janis Beresford-McLennan

Outskirts Press, Inc.
Denver, Colorado

MEGAN
All Rights Reserved.
Copyright © 2010 Janis Beresford-McLennan
v4.0 r1.2

Cover image by Catherine Wise

Outskirts Press, Inc.
http://www.outskirtspress.com

ISBN: 978-1-4327-5727-4

Outskirts Press and the "OP" logo are trademarks belonging to Outskirts Press, Inc.

PRINTED IN THE UNITED STATES OF AMERICA

I want to thank my Teacher. He has given me the skills and ability to write. He is My Counselor. He gives me inspiration and golden opportunities.

Chapter 1

Megan admired herself in the full-length mirror. She was a vision of loveliness to behold. "Wow! You look beautiful," whispered Lizzie as she helped her best friend with her veil.

In a few minutes, Megan would be walking down the aisle on her father's arm and waiting at the altar will be the most perfect man in the world, Tom Brinkley.

Tom was an anesthesiologist at Crestview General Hospital. Every woman's head would turn in his direction whenever he walked into the room. He was popular, tall, slim and blonde. His ice blue eyes were unreadable but his charming smile was winning. Megan was envied by many of the women who knew Tom and she was told over and over how lucky she was to be marrying this gorgeous specimen of a man.

There was a knock at the door and Megan said, "Come in"

Joan Garrison entered the room where her daughter Megan and maid of honor, Lizzie were getting dressed. Joan gave Megan a critical look and said, "It's time to leave for the church. This is the day we were all waiting for. Be good to that man. Remember, there are many women who would give anything to be in your shoes!" Joan was on a mission to make sure this wedding was perfect. She had successfully orchestrated this marriage and was very pleased with herself. She stood by the window looking down at the street below. The limousine arrived to take Megan to the church. Her mind strayed for a moment as she reflected on her humble beginnings twenty-seven years ago.

Joan was a sophisticated, brown skinned, African American woman who didn't have a college degree. She didn't graduate high school but you wouldn't know it. She was well read and had perfect diction. Many people told her that she looked like Diane Carroll, the actress.

On her eighteenth birthday, Joan took the $250.00 she saved up from doing errands for people in her neighborhood. She used the money from gifts and wherever she could grab a dollar and ran as fast as she could, leaving the life she hated and her family behind.

Joan arrived in the small town of Crestview Falls determined never to return to her old lifestyle. She wanted a new beginning and she was going to make it happen. The cheapest place she could find to stay was a motel four blocks away from Crestview General Hospital. The very next day Joan walked up to the hospital seeking employment. The clerk in Human Resources who processed her paperwork sent her down to housekeeping for an interview with the supervisor.

Peter Garrison was a nice looking twenty-eight year old Caucasian of medium height with a very quiet personality. He liked Joan very much. She looked and acted much older than eighteen and he hired her on the spot. He explained her duties to her.

"This job isn't glamorous, it's hard work. You have to clean patient rooms, hallways, staff offices, then empty the trash bins, sweep and mop floors. What do you think? Still want the job?" The visual and mental opinion that he was forming about this young woman did not fit that kind of work at all. The stately way in which she carried herself and her eloquent speech drew instant admiration and respect. She looked like she belonged in one of the executive offices, not in housekeeping.

"I can handle it. Just you watch. I'll be the best employee you ever hired. I promise." Despite the nature of these tasks, when Joan arrived for work in the morning she could have easily been mistaken for an executive. She always wore a perfectly tailored suit and would change into her uniform to perform her duties. When her day was complete she would change back into her suit and go home.

She kept her promise. She took great pride in her work. She studied the hospital staff and the patients. She spoke to everyone cheerfully and catered to their needs. Soon everyone knew and respected her. She and Peter became a team and he depended heavily on her. Joan had not only reorganized his office and staff, but housekeeping was run more efficiently.

Peter admired Joan and began to develop feelings for her. Joan had just finished her shift and they were leaving at the same time. He was shy and didn't know how to ask her for a date. So he awkwardly began a conversation with her.

"I know that you had a very busy day but you don't look a bit tired. Would you like to grab a bite to eat?"

"Are you asking me out on a date?"

"Well, it's dinner time and we're both hungry, so if that's a date, yes."

"I'd be delighted to go to dinner with you."

They had a good time that evening and began dating.

Peter came from a loving family. They didn't have a lot of money and because of that Joan had mixed feelings about them. She didn't like or disliked them. Her friends and acquaintances were carefully picked; they were rich or at least middle class. She studied rich people and planned to live exactly as they did.

After a brief period of dating, Peter and Joan decided to get married. He lived with his parents because he was saving to buy his own home. Being as savvy as she was, Joan agreed with Peter's plan to use the money to buy their first home. She decided she and Peter would go to the Justice of the Peace to marry alone, but his family insisted on being present for their son's wedding. After the ceremony the newlyweds, Peter's parents and his older sister Marcia lunched at one of the best restaurants to celebrate.

Peter and Joan moved to a small suburban neighborhood that she picked, just outside of the city. Lined along the streets were picture perfect homes with professionally manicured lawns. Joan excitedly began to decorate her new home choosing the very best. Two months into the marriage she became pregnant. Life was good, nowhere close to what she had envisioned, but it was a good start.

———«◍»———

As time passed, Peter began to notice his wife's insensitive ways but he attributed it to her youthfulness. What bothered him the most was her ruthless ambition. The way she pushed and manipulated every situation in her quest for success. Joan positioned herself in the right social circles. She belonged to the right charitable and political organizations and connected with key people.

Chapter 2

Nine months later, Joan gave birth to a baby girl she named Megan. The Garrisons were excited to see their first grandchild and rushed to the hospital to see the baby. After his family left the hospital, Peter settled down and held his new baby girl close. He looked admiringly at his daughter. "Isn't she beautiful?"

Joan was very upset, but Peter thought she was just tired after giving birth. "Peter, what happened to her? I thought that she would look white!"

"Joan, she is a healthy, beautiful, little girl and that's all that matters."

"You don't know anything. Look at her fingers!"

Peter checked Megan's fingers. "They look perfect to me?"

"You see that darker coloration above her nails? That's the color she'll be. She should have been much fairer! I am light and you are white. She should look white!"

"Joan, what does it matter? I can barely see any color there anyway. The color above her fingernail is very light. There are white people with that complexion. Why are you so prejudice against your own race? I don't understand it."

She ignored her husband's question, even if she tried to explain he wouldn't understand. She thought back to the world she came from. A world where black was ugly. The women she knew were on welfare, pregnant most of the time, and neglected their kids. The men were either gone, abusive, cheaters, or substance abusers. Her father deserted her before she was born and left her to suffer. He didn't give a damn about her. No, Peter wouldn't understand. Instead she changed the subject. "Listen, I applied for the office manager position and I got the job. I start in two weeks."

"What? Joan! Aren't you going to take your maternity leave? What about the baby?"

"I have looked into daycare and found one that will enroll babies her age."

Peter was upset and didn't like the idea of Megan being cared for by strangers at such a young age. "My God Joan! You haven't left the hospital yet and you already have the child in daycare?"

Joan was highly annoyed, "Peter, the responsibility of this position is not only for housekeeping but running the entire office staff! *You* should have applied for it but you didn't. I've gotten used to your laid-back attitude on the job and I have often had to take things into my own hands. I am *not* going to let some stranger get that position! You deserve that promotion and if you are not going to climb the corporate ladder, I most *certainly* will."

"Do what you want. You usually do anyway."

The next day the Garrisons were back for a visit with their new grandchild. Happy faces beamed and the entire conversation was about the beautiful baby that had entered their lives. Marcia noticed that her sister-in-law had bandaged her breast and that the baby was being bottle-fed. Peter had confided in her about the daycare situation and Marcia had an idea that she wanted to speak to the family about. "Joan, when are you returning to work?"

Joan didn't think it was any of Marcia's business, but in the spirit of things, she decided to be polite and answer her. "In two weeks." She was expecting criticism or some kind of negative remark but instead, Marcia said, "I have an idea that I would like you and Peter to consider."

Joan looked hesitantly at her husband, but held her tongue. "What is it?"

"Mom complains constantly that she hates her job, and how tired she is of working. She can take early retirement. She has the years of service, then she can be Megan's nanny."

Joan liked the idea, and Peter was grateful that Megan would be in a loving environment. They hadn't heard from Rose and from the look on her face, this was the first time she had heard of this. They all looked in her direction for an answer, but Peter Sr. answered. "Honey, I know that you would be thrilled to take care of the baby."

"Yes, I think it's a great idea, but I have to check on my benefits. I'll go into personnel tomorrow and I'll have an answer for you by the end of this week." It seemed the best situation for everyone and after Rose found out that her benefits were not going to be compromised in any way, she retired and took on the job of caring for Megan.

After two weeks at home, Joan was going out of her mind and was eager to begin her new job. She worked late into the night and on weekends, but always picked up her child at the end of day, no matter how late.

Marcia helped her mother with Megan when she got home from work and on the weekends. She enjoyed her role as Aunt. She fed Megan dinner, gave her baths, read books to her, and played with her. She would cuddle with Megan until Joan came to pick her up.

The relationship between Joan and Peter began to deteriorate. Peter became passive and threw himself into his work while his family parented Megan. Megan's education was very important to Joan. She did the research and found the most prestigious and the best kindergarten program for Megan. She took the day off and eagerly took Megan to school. She made sure that administration knew that she was Megan's mother and that they were accountable to her for Megan's progress. That day a very secure and confident Megan met Jennifer Dupree, Lizzie Conrad and Ariel Rosen, and this little group became best friends. Later they found out that they were neighbors.

As Megan grew, it was always she, Grandpa, Grandma Rose, and Aunt Marcia. They were devoted to each other and Megan grew to be a beautiful child. Joan never seemed to mind when her in-laws took Megan to Disney or to children plays. Megan loved to sit on Grandpa's lap and share his meals with him and ride around on his shoulders. Marcia changed her schedule to accommodate taking Megan to music lessons, dance classes, horseback riding, and spending time with her on the weekends. They did everything that a mother and daughter would do. Megan received unconditional love from her father's family. She was a happy and delightful child.

Although Joan had no intention of spending that kind of time that the family did with her daughter, she seemed jealous of Megan's love and adoration for them.

Megan was very wise and a good little housekeeper. She cooked, cleaned, and maintained the peace in their home. Joan was gone most of the time either at work or at one of her organizational functions. Peter worked to keep himself busy and they provided their child the best lifestyle that money had to offer especially a first class education. Joan insisted on disciplining the child and she made sure that Megan's grades were always excellent. The years passed quickly and Megan grew into a lovely young lady and was accepted at Princeton. She came home every chance she got because she missed her family and Rose and Marcia made every visit very special. Peter became more passive and since he had no need to pretend for Megan's sake that the marriage was a happy one he moved into the guest room.

Chapter 3

Megan graduated from Princeton with her Masters degree in Theatrical Arts with a major in Cinematography. She applied for a job and was getting dressed for her first interview and sought help from her mother. She held up two suits, "Mama, which one?"

"Megan, it doesn't matter what you wear, you won't get anywhere in that profession. It's a man's world. You could have been a physician or an attorney but no. You've been carrying around that damn camera all your life! I rue the day I let you talk me into buying all that camera equipment. I thought that it was just a hobby and you would get over it."

Megan disregarded her mother's comments and continued to go on interviews. Joan was more interested in marrying her daughter off. Joan met Tom Brinkley at the hospital, he came down to her office with a complaint and they hit it off right away. He was courteous, respectful, and very thoughtful. He got preferred treatment from Joan's staff because she respected him. His office was well furnished and every item he requested was immediately delivered and in return he would bring Joan breakfast, take her out to lunch or send her flowers. He was always doing something nice for her. She decided that she wanted him for Megan and began to spark his interest every chance she got. He was a nice young man, good looking, and most importantly he was white. She could just imagine her beautiful white grandchildren. So Joan decided to invite Tom to dinner with the family.

Joan entered the living room, leaned up against the television and folded her arms. Glaring at Peter she sarcastically says, "Peter, I've invited a very nice young man to dinner. I'd like you to be here and I need you to act like a husband and father. Do you think that you can handle that?"

Peter shrugged and continued reading his newspaper. Immediately her attention was turned to Megan who had just gotten off the phone with her grandmother. "Megan as I was saying to your father, I've invited a very nice young man to dinner. He is a very important physician at the hospital, so please be mindful and don't disappoint me."

Peter lowered the paper and commented: "Here she goes again, fixing people's lives. Megan run before you get caught in your mother's trap."

Joan was annoyed, "She would be lucky if he is the least interested in her. You don't have any eligible bachelors knocking our door down, do you? Let's see what you have to wear?" She and Megan began walking towards Megan's room discussing her plans for the evening. "Did your grandparents say what time they are going to be here? I hope that they are on time because this dinner is really important to me."

"No, we didn't talk about your dinner but grandma is always on time. You're the one that's always late, remember?"

Completely ignoring Megan, Joan walked into Megan's closet and began to pick out a dress she thought would be appropriate.

Megan pulled the dress away from her. "Mama, you do know that I am dating Samuel and I really like him."

Joan retrieved the dress from Megan and with a disgusted look on her face, spoke sternly. "Megan he has got nothing to offer you or anyone else for that matter. You had better get your head out of the gutter. You need to scrape all the black off of you. Thank God you're fair and you've got good hair. I don't want any ugly little children calling me grandma or Big Mama or whatever the hell they say."

Megan sarcastically said, "You mean ugly little *black* children, don't you?"

Joan gave her a knowing look, "Honey, all that relationship has for you is lots of babies, section 8 housing riddled with roaches, and the joy of waiting for your next welfare check to come."

Disdainfully Megan replied, "Mama, sometimes you can be so hateful! Why do you say such horrible things about people you don't even know? Samuel comes from a very educated and well-grounded family. His parents have been married for thirty-five years. His father is the CEO of his own company, for crying out loud! I'll have you know that his mother is an attorney for one of the most prestigious firms in the United States. Samuel is a teacher and he is a really nice guy."

" Nice Guy? You think I don't know him? I know men like him. They are lazy! They don't want to work! Can't keep a damn job and they make terrible parents that don't show up for their kids half the time! If you want to find them, go to a bar or to a street corner. It baffles me to know where they get the money from for the liquor and drugs but they can't buy a pot to piss in. They live like hogs in a pigsty. What's the matter with you? We live in a town with very prominent white people. You went to an all white school, the best in the county. I sent you away to an Ivy League University and you found the only black family that lives in this town to consort with."

"But Mama, you're black!"

"Don't remind me! And why do you keep calling me Mama? I hate it!"

"For your information, I'm very proud of who I am, *Mama*"

"Child, please! That's been done. The 'I'm black and I'm proud' movement was in the seventies. They're still black and too damn proud to get a good job and keep it. Tom is a Physician! Are you listening to me? He is an Anesthesiologist the best in his field. He comes from a very wealthy family. the Brinkleys are old money. He makes good money. You will have a wonderful life with a great man. You will have beautiful children and they will have a good future." She picked up the dress and shoved it into Megan's hand. "Here wear this." Joan walked out of Megan's room and slammed the door behind her.

Megan hugged the dress as she sat on her bed thinking; *I wonder what happened to Mama that makes her hate being black so bad. I'm gonna go to her stupid dinner so that she will leave me alone.*

———— ◉ ————

Later that evening she got dressed and went down to dinner and behaved as Joan requested. The dinner went well but her mother wasn't satisfied. Megan seemed totally disinterested in Tom. When Joan kept pressing the issue of Megan and Tom dating, Megan had the audacity to mention Samuel. What was Joan going to do about Samuel Watson? She had to find a way to get rid of him. Joan decided to speak frankly to Samuel, so she called him.

"Hello?"

"Samuel, this is Joan Garrison."

"Mrs. Garrison, is Megan okay?"

"She's fine. Samuel I would like to meet with you and have a talk but I don't want you to tell Megan about our meeting."

"Okay Mrs. Garrison, when do you want us to meet?"

"Tomorrow afternoon after work would be best. I'll meet you at Ruby's on Ninth and Lexington." Joan hated that dreadful place. She figured it would please Samuel, of course he'd want to eat chicken! Besides, it would soften the blow.

"See you then."

The next day Joan and Samuel met at Ruby's. The waitress smacking her gum was ready to take their order. She looked at Joan, rolled her eyes, and said, "Wha'd ya having?"

Joan ignored her and said to Samuel, "I would like a club soda, please."

Amused, Samuel smiled at the waitress and says, I'll have a beer.

The waitress said, "Right away *Madame*" and left to fill the order.

"Samuel, I'll get right to the point. Megan is dating a doctor."

"Dating? I thought – "

Joan interrupted him, "He is a very nice guy and they are getting serious but she is afraid of hurting your feelings."

"I don't understand. Megan never told me – "

She interrupted him again. "I want to ask you to bow out of her life gracefully. If you care for her you will allow her to move on with her life."

A look of disbelief appeared on his face but he was not sure she was telling the truth. "If Megan doesn't want to see me anymore all she has to do is say so."

"Samuel, you know Megan. She is a sweet and caring person and would hate to hurt your feelings and that is why I am here. I want to spare the two of you an awkward situation. This is what I want you to do. I want you to tell her that you think that the two of you need to see other people for a while and if in a year or so the two of you still want to be together then you'll find your way. If what she feels for you is love, it will last."

The waitress returned with Samuel's beer and what appeared to be grape soda. Joan looked at the soda and then at the waitress saying, "I believe I ordered *club soda* not *grape soda*."

The waitress spits back at her, "Lady, this is Ruby's Chicken and Waffles. This is not the Hard Rock Café" and she walked away.

Samuel solemnly said, "I want what is best for Megan. I'll do what you ask."

Joan pushed the grape soda to the side and agreed, "Good, I knew that I could count on you."

That night Samuel broke up with Megan.

⸺ ◦⟨◉⟩◦ ⸺

Joan stormed into her living room where Megan was watching television from the couch. "Megan, I saw Tom today in the cafeteria and he said that he called you and you failed to return his call. I did not teach you to be rude." She handed Megan the phone. "Here! Call him now!" Megan always tried to be good for Joan. She craved her mother's love and approval. Even though she was feeling sad from her break-up with Samuel, she made the call and Tom invited her to a movie and dinner. Tom arrived promptly on time and Megan was not ready so he waited. Megan finally appeared. "Hi Tom, I'm sorry to keep you waiting."

He seemed irritated yet diplomatic about it. "That's alright." He walked her to the car and opened the door for her.

She said, "Thank you." and she sat down. He got into the drivers seat and they were on their way when she said, "Tom I hope you don't mind but I would prefer if we split the bill." She could see the muscle in his jaw contract as he replied.

"When I take a woman out, *I* pay the bill."

"I know but I would feel better if I paid my way."

Tom gripped the steering wheel, takes a deep breath and says, "It's settled! When you're with me I'll pay. Why don't you sit back and enjoy the evening."

Megan decided to take his advice. She enjoyed the movie and then they went to the restaurant where the food was superb. After they were finished eating the main course, the waiter asked, "Would you like to see the desert menu?" Tom immediately said, "No." Without consulting Megan. It was enough that he ordered her meal for her. She didn't like him making the decision whether or not she had desert but she kept her cool. She felt that it was a simple thing and although he seemed a bit controlling he was a nice guy. In spite of their little difference of opinion, they had a good time. He was the perfect gentleman and she enjoyed being with him.

Joan couldn't wait for Megan to get home. She was excited and waited up to hear how the date went.

"Well, tell me. How did it go?"

"Mom, why are you still up? I thought you had to get up early for work?"

"I'll manage. Go on, tell me how your date with Tom went."

"It was okay."

"Okay? Okay? I spend all my time fixing things for you to have an okay date?"

"Well, he was a gentleman but I didn't like that he insisted on paying the bill, he ordered the steamed fish for me, you know I don't really like fish and he refused to even look at the desert menu. It made me feel a bit uncomfortable."

"Uncomfortable! Tom is a man of great means. He took you out, insisted on paying the bill, suggested the best meal and you're upset? Megan this man is experienced. He grew up dining in fine restaurants and he knows what is best. Honey, why can't you relax and enjoy yourself? You are being ridiculous. I'm going to bed. Goodnight, get some sleep." To Joan's delight Tom's interest grew and became intense. Before long, Megan and Tom were dating exclusively.

Megan opened the front door to the house without any enthusiasm. She was exhausted after having what had to have been the worst job interview of her life. She walked into the living room throwing her keys on the coffee table. She was drained and all she wanted to do was curl up in her bed and forget this whole day ever happened. Instead, she needed to be getting ready for dinner with Tom and her parents. She really liked Tom but she wasn't sure about their relationship yet. She was so deep in her own thoughts that she didn't even notice the large bouquet of flowers until she almost bumped into them. "Mama, are you here?"

"Back in the bedroom, Megan."

Megan made her way to her mom's room.

"How did that interview go today?"

"Ugh, awful. I don't want to talk about it. Who sent you flowers?"

"They're for you, from Tom."

"Wow, they're really beautiful, it's just what I needed to put me in a better mood. Tom is really thoughtful."

Joan beamed, "See! I told you. Come zip me up."

Megan zipped up the black cocktail dress her mother was wearing, "You look great, Mama."

"Of course I do. You need to run along and get yourself dressed. Tom will be here soon and we don't need him seeing you looking a mess. Hurry!"

"I'm going, I'm going." Megan went to her room and as she got dressed she wondered why Tom needed to impress her entire family. He was pushing the relationship along quickly and he seemed to want everyone's approval, everyone but her. Twenty minutes later, she had finished dressing and went into the living room where Tom was waiting.

Admiringly he complimented them, "Wow! You look great. I am in the company of the two most terrific looking women in Crestview Falls." With the biggest smile on her face Joan hurried them out the door.

The restaurant was downtown on Michigan Avenue. The Valet took the car and they all walked in and were seated immediately. The host spoke to Tom as if he were a VIP customer. The restaurant was elegant. Megan's entire family including her grandparents and Marcia were there. Everyone was having a wonderful time, but Megan wondered what the big to-do was about. The food was delicious and everything was done to perfection. Then Tom ordered the most expensive bottle of Champagne. When it arrived and everyone held a glass of Champagne in their hands, Tom got down on one knee.

"Megan, will you marry me?"

Megan was surprised, but she smiled trying to hide it. She

knew right away that her mother had known all along that Tom was planning to propose. Her hand went up to her mouth and Tom waited. His face was serious and it was clear he expected an immediate answer. She caught her breath and said, "Yes!"

With that he placed a five Carat diamond engagement ring on her ring finger. He pulled her close to him and kissed her while everyone in the restaurant clapped. Tom stood up and bowed to his audience. "Thank you. Thank you."

They drank to the happy couple. Joan was in her element, but the rest of the family were silent participants and made every effort to be happy for Megan. Rose didn't know exactly why she had that anxious feeling in her stomach but she guarded it and smiled. Her husband and daughter felt the same way. They had discussed their reservations about Tom before, but none of them could come up with exactly what they disliked about him. Something was just off. They all could see the wheels turning in Joan's head. Joan turned to Tom. "Tom, what about your folks? Are they going to come for the wedding?"

Tom took a sip of champagne and nonchalantly said, "I don't think so. They are currently living in Europe. They hate living here and don't visit often. My father is not in good health and my mom never leaves him." Tom put his hand on Megan's, "But I will take my lovely bride to see them soon."

Joan felt compassion for him, "I'm sorry to hear about your dad but I hate planning this wedding without them."

"Believe me they won't mind. I will make sure that they meet Megan later."

Images of flower arrangements and wedding gowns danced in Joan's head. "Okay I will make the plans. Umm, how about June next year? Megan what do you think?"

Things were going fast but Megan didn't want to upset her mother.

She hated when Joan was angry with her. "Mama that sounds great!"

Tom butted in. "Sorry girls, I can't wait that long. How about next month?"

"Next month!?" Was the unanimous cry of everyone at the table.

"Yes. I believe that is what I said."

Even Joan was surprised in Tom's haste to get married. "Tom, I cannot possibly plan a wedding in thirty days. It would be near impossible to do all that needs to be done. We have to --"

Before she finished her sentence, Tom said, "Joan you and I both know that you can accomplish anything you want to and I'm confident that you can get it all done in time. For God's sake this is 1998."

She raised her champagne glass and with a confident smile she concurred. "When you are right, you are right. I sure can, and I will." Joan had orchestrated the entire romance and was very pleased with herself as well as the outcome.

Tom's cell phone rang at that moment. It was the hospital and he had to go. He beckoned the waiter, "I have to leave. Here is my card, please make sure that the tab is paid." The waiter returned his credit card and Tom kissed his fiancée, said goodnight and left.

Rose took this opportunity to speak to Megan. "Megan honey, are you sure this is what you want? It seems kind of quick. Honey, please think about what you are about to do. Marriage is a serious matter."

Joan was angry. *Who does Rose think she is?* She was Megan's mother. "Rose, Megan is fine. Look at her, she is beaming with joy."

Rose didn't want to rain on her granddaughter's parade but her reservations about Tom kept nagging at her. One thing for sure she disliked his arrogance.

Chapter 4

Megan had four close friends. Lizzie lived next door, Jennifer and Ariel lived a few houses away and Megan met Kenny in college. Kenny now owned a nightclub and performed in several of the shows as a drag queen by the name *Lulu,* which he preferred to be called. They hadn't seen Megan since she began dating Tom but finally got in touch with her. They planned to meet at Crestview Hill Restaurant. Megan walked into the restaurant and her friends waved to her. "Hi! We're over here."

She walked over to where they were. "Hi!" They hugged and kissed each other and then sat down. "Guys, I'm sorry that I haven't been able to return your calls. I've been so busy job hunting and Tom ---"

Before she could finish Lulu said, "Is that a rock I see on your finger? Wow! How many carats? No, don't tell me. I'd say five. Am I right?"

Megan nodded and very quietly said, "Tom and I got engaged last week. Here are the pictures."

There was a hush at the table as they passed the pictures around to each other. Ariel asked, "Where did you meet him?"

And Megan said, "He's an anesthesiologist at Crestview General. My mom introduced us.

Jennifer tossed her long blond hair back, looked at the picture Lulu passed to her and with an attitude said, "Joan finally found you a man, huh" She smirked and said, "And look he's white."

Megan was red in the face. Jennifer had touched a raw nerve. "You're just jealous. You have always been jealous of me. It's not my fault that your father left before you were born or that your mom drank herself to sleep at night. You need to get a life and find someone to love you. I found a wonderful man and I'm getting married. I was going to ask you to be my maid of honor but I'll save you the trouble. You don't have to be my maid of honor. You don't even have to be at my wedding."

Jennifer was stunned at Megan's attitude. They had never had a disagreement like this before. The others had heard enough.

Lulu was concerned for his friend and he asked, "Megan honey, Isn't it a bit soon? You and Tom have only known each other for three months. Oh my God, are you pregnant?"

"No Lulu, I'm not pregnant. Tom and I want to spend the rest of our lives together and we don't see why we should have to wait"

"Megan honey, all I'm saying is that you need more time to get to know each other. That's all. I really think you are rushing and you shouldn't."

Megan was on the defensive but she loved Lulu and respected his opinion. "Lulu, I'm not rushing anything and by the way the wedding is next month."

"Next Month! Oh honey, that's quick."

Megan did not respond to Lulu's comment, instead she spoke to Lizzie. "Lizzie will you be my maid of honor?"

Lizzie was caught by surprise but didn't want to offend her friend. "Sure Megan."

"Thank you. I'll call you later with the details. Megan was still upset and didn't want to be with her friends any longer so she made polite excuses and left but Jennifer was still fuming.

"I'm not jealous. Don't you think it's strange that none of us have even met Tom?" She looked at everyone at the table.

Lulu was silently mulling things over in his head and was very concerned for his friend. He said, "Look's like our friend is defending her decision to get married too much. Don't you think?"

Ariel agreed. "Lulu, I was thinking the very same thing. It's not like Megan. Why has she kept us from meeting him? And why is she so defensive?"

Lizzie said, " Jen, you were just wrong. Why did you have to be so nasty? Look we're her friends and we'll do what we always do. We'll be there for her, agreed?"

They all said, "Agreed."

Megan returned home. The house was in darkness and she tiredly walked up to the front door. She opened the door when she heard a voice that came from the dark corner of the patio.

"Where have you been?"

She jumped. It was Tom. "Tom what are you doing here?"

"You didn't answer me? Where were you?"

"Tom not now."

Tom was now standing beside her. He held her arm firmly. "I asked you a question and I want an answer. I've been calling you the past three hours and you didn't answer your phone."

Megan wriggled her arm free. "I was with my friends. I wanted to tell them about the wedding."

His voice became tender. "Megan I'm sorry. You know how much I love you. It makes me crazy when I can't get in touch with you."

"Well I'm here now."

"Yes, you are." Tom drew her close and kissed her passionately.

Chapter 5

Joan was eagerly planning the most elegant wedding she could in such a short time frame.

"Joan have you seen these bills? This wedding is costing us a fortune!"

"Peter, do you know who will be in attendance? The Mayor, the Governor, and the very elite of this town. You have to spend money when you are entertaining the best."

"The best?" He shook his head is disbelief at his wife's desire to impress people that she didn't even know very well. Joan wanted the absolute best. She had to keep up appearances. Everybody that was anybody was invited to the wedding. It was the event of the year in Crestview Falls.

Joan said to Megan, "I had the invitations hand delivered because we don't have time to mail them. I hope Rose and Marcia dress properly. Maybe you can help them to find something appropriate."

"Mama, Grandma dresses very well. She may not wear designer clothing, but she looks good to me. Aunt Marcia always looks cute too. You need to stop." Megan stopped every attempt Joan made to demean her father's family. Most of her cherished childhood memories included them. She didn't know her mother's side of the family. There were times she wondered about them but knew not to broach the subject and as every other event in her life, none of them were invited to the wedding.

Chapter 6

A nervous Megan walked with her father down the aisle of the cathedral. There at the altar stood her handsome fiance and his smile told her everything she wanted to know. He loved her. Megan was a bit sad because she wanted Jennifer, her closest friend, to be her maid of honor but they hadn't seen each other or spoken since the terrible fight that night.

On her way to the altar she looked to her left and there sat Jennifer. She blew a kiss Megan's way and mouthed, *I'm sorry*. A great big smile framed Megan's face and she mouthed back, *I'm sorry and I love you*. Her day could not be more perfect. Tom and Megan said their vows and after an extravagant wedding reception they left for their honeymoon in Hawaii.

⸺⬧⸺

An exhausted Joan sat at her dining room table massaging her aching feet. She said to her husband, "That was a beautiful wedding, wasn't it?"

"It sure cost us enough. I would have been upset if it weren't.

"Peter, is there anything that I do that you are not unhappy about?"

He shrugged his shoulder and without another word he went to bed.

Chapter 7

Tom and Megan landed in Hawaii, ready for their honeymoon. The honeymoon suite at the hotel was luxuriously decorated. On a table in the living room were a huge bouquet of flowers, a fruit basket, and a complimentary bottle of Champagne that Tom eagerly opened.

Megan got dressed in anticipation of a romantic evening. She wore a white negligee and matching white wedge heeled bedroom slippers. She was a beautiful young woman. Her curly hair flowed to her waist. Megan sported a natural look that many women paid their hairdresser handsomely for. Her fair complexion was flawless but her beautiful facial features revealed the magnificence of her biracial ethnicity. Her eyebrows were perfectly shaped over the most brilliant black eyes. Her nose was not straight but it was cute and complemented luscious plump lips. She had a perfectly shaped body. D cups, a small waist, nice round hips, a cute butt, again revealing her ethnic background, and a pair of the most sexy legs. She was a very attractive bi-racial woman who proudly called herself black.

Tom was already in bed. "What took you so long?"

She smiled shyly. "I wanted to be beautiful for my new husband."

He pulled her to him and kissed her forcefully. His kisses were rough. He ripped off her clothes and proceeded to roughly make love to her. He sucked on her breast and then he bit them. "Oww, Tom that hurts!" Her comments went on deaf ears. He spread her legs and he entered. This was not what she expected but she wanted to make him happy. She responded timidly to his strides. He was completely satisfied after a quick minute, but there was no pleasure in it for her.

"Where did you learn to have sex like that?"

"What are you talking about? I was just trying to please you. I am a virgin."

"Virgin? Honey, you can screw with the best of them."

"Tom. I swear, I never had sex before."

He turned over and went to sleep. She tossed and turned most of the night and silent tears streamed down the side of her face but she was determined to make her husband happy. The next morning she got up and ordered breakfast. She had a shower and was ready to start a romantic day. She thought about last night. *Maybe she had imagined the events of the evening before. She did drink two glasses of champagne. Tom was a kind and gentle man. He loved her and had always seen to her needs. She misjudged what happened. That's it. It didn't really happen the way she remembered.* She went to him. "Wake up sleepy head breakfast is here."

" I'm not asleep."

She kissed him softly and she said. "I love you."

He grabbed her hair and pushed her head down. "Go down."

"What?"

"I said go down." He grabbed her head harder and he pushed her down between his legs. "Go on do it."

She was crying and in a trembling voice she said, "Tom you're hurting me. Do what?"

"Don't act stupid. You know what to do. I am sure that you've done it several times."

She was awkward, She did not know what to do but she tried. *What is happening? How can this be? This is not the man I married, she thought.*

"Okay, if you want me to I'll tell you what to do. Maybe that's what turns you on." He told her in detail what he wanted her to do to him. The more pleasure he got the harder he grabbed her hair almost tearing it off her head. She did as he demanded. The putrid smell of his unwashed crotch made her nauseated. She tried to hold her breath while she hastily performed this vile act and he held her head down until he was satisfied. "That was good." He let go of her head and he got up. He slapped her on her rear end. "I am starving."

As soon as she could muster the strength, she ran to the bath-room and she stuck her finger down her throat and she began to vomit. She cleaned her teeth several times and then she took another bath. She was numb and in a daze. She wanted to wake up from this nightmare. She now knew that she didn't imagine what happened the night before. She was confused. *No one changes overnight. Not like this.* She battled in her mind searching for clues but couldn't find any at the moment. Finally she got dressed and came outside. He acted as if nothing happened and in a happy carefree way he said.

"Sorry I couldn't wait. I was hungry. Breakfast was good. Want to go sightseeing?"

Confused, she tried to act natural. She said, "Ah -- Yes ---I'll get my camera and my bag. I want to take lots of pictures."

"You and that damn camera. Half the luggage was your camera equipment."

It was a gorgeous day in Hawaii and Tom was his usual thoughtful self. They actually had fun. They laughed and played like they did while they were dating. They strolled down the beach and he bought her flowers and gifts to take back home. It was a perfect day. As she showered for dinner she thought to herself, *he's back. It won't happen again. My loving Tom is back.*

That night they went to a very nice restaurant for dinner. While they were eating, a man at the table across from them suspected that they were honeymooners and sent a bottle of Champagne over to their table. When the waiter pointed him out to them as the person who sent it, the man smiled at Megan and lifted his glass in an attempt to toast the newlyweds. She wrote a note and showed it to her husband before she gave it to the waiter. It said, *My husband and I thank you.* They laughed and talked and had a good time and then left to go back to the hotel. Megan was just about to get ready for bed and out of nowhere she felt a hot sting on her cheek and her head snapped back. Her body shook from the unexpected slap across her face. Through clinched teeth Tom said, "Who was that? Did you invite your man on our honeymoon?"

"Tom, What is the matter with you? I don't know that man! I don't have any other man, I love you!"

"Sure you do! You're nothing but a slut!"

Megan was paralyzed with fear and she wailed in agony.

"Please Tom don't hurt me. Please, I love you, only you."

He grabbed her hair and rubbed her face into the carpet until she got carpet burn. He pushed her into the wall and threw her onto the furniture. He kicked her and he beat her until she couldn't move. The room was a mess. Megan lay on the floor that night while her husband snored on a king size bed in their honeymoon suite. She wanted to know *why, why was he acting this way? What did she do? What could she do to make things the way they were before they got married?*

―――――――――

The next two days he took care of her bruises. "Megan, why did you make me hurt you? You shouldn't make me so mad. You make me crazy. Here, let me put this on your face." He placed ice packs on her bruises and he had the most gentle touch. The days that followed were very pleasant. It was day four of their vacation and Tom stood on the veranda of the hotel for a while and then he returned inside. "Honey lets go swimming. The beach looks inviting."

"Okay." She went to her suitcase and she picked up the beautiful bikini she bought especially for this trip. She got scared. The past two days were good and today started out calm, she didn't want to ruin it by sending him into a jealous rage. He leaned into the bedroom and through the door he called. "Are you ready?"

"In a minute." She appeared in a pair of jeans and an oversized top. He gave her a surprised look. "I don't feel like going into the water but I'll sit and watch you."

"Don't be silly. Go on change, we will have fun in the sea, and you can bring your camera and take as many pictures as you want."

"Tom I didn't bring a proper bathing suit. I meant to buy one but I didn't. I have one that Lizzie lent me and I don't think I want to wear it. Tom I really don't want to go into the water. I have this book that I have been meaning to read. All of my friends are talking about it. They say that it is a nice read. I'll just sit and read."

He smiled that charming smile that bottled his rage. "I'll let you get away with it this time. Let's go." They went to the beach and they rented a big umbrella and chairs. She sat and read while Tom swam and ran back occasionally to check on her. They had lunch and it was a nice day until a very handsome guy smiled and spoke to Megan. He said, "Are you sick? Why are you hiding that gorgeous body?" She kept her head down, fear grabbed her and the tears emerged and silently rolled down her cheeks. Her heart pounded and sweat covered her body. Terrified, she began to shake while Tom eyed her, "Are you ready to go back to our room?"

"Yes Tom, I am."

They returned to their suite and she was waiting for the beating she knew was coming, but Tom showered and sat down to watch television until dinner. Her stomach churned and fear gripped her insides. She waited and waited. Imaginary thoughts tormented her mind. *When will he strike? How will he strike?* She had no idea what would set him off. He ordered room service, they ate dinner and they stayed in. He came close to her and he reached over. She jumped and cowered. "What's the matter with you? I was just going to check that black eye of yours. It should have started to fade by now." He got an ice-cold towel and he pressed it gently. "That guy who spoke to you today felt sorry for you. You're lucky that I love you. You'll never be able to find another man like me. I take care of you, don't I?"

"Yes Tom, you do and I am very grateful."

"Megan, nobody wants you. Not even your parents. It was the happiest day in your mother's life when I proposed to you and your father doesn't give a damn either way. You should be grateful that I married you." He kissed her on her forehead. "No one could ever love you like I do. Go lie down and get a good night's rest. Let's see how it looks in the morning." The psychological game had begun. The next morning they had normal sex. She was so scared that she was unable to enjoy it. However, she realized that she had better pretend.

There were no more incidents while they were on their honeymoon. She was showered with gifts but Megan was completely stressed out. She had no idea what would set him off. The time to return home had come and Megan was eager to return to the safety of her family and friends. They arrived home and the next day Tom went to work and Megan sought the comfort of her family.

Chapter 8

Megan went to visit her parents at work. "Hi Daddy." She kissed him on the cheek. "I need to see you in Mama's office." He walked with her to Joan's office.

"Hi honey, you're back. Tell me you had a great time. I hope we got our money's worth. Your father paid for that honeymoon out of his own pocket." She searched Megan's face and her eyes were filled with curiosity. "Where are the pictures? I know that you took a ton of them, Ms. Movie Director."

"Mama, Daddy, I have to tell you something. Tom hit me. Look."

She stripped down to her underwear to show them the severe bruises. Peter nodded his head and said to his wife,

"Joan, I want you to take a good look at your daughter's torso! I told you that he wasn't who he pretended to be! I told you that there was something off about him but no you wouldn't listen. You told me to stay out of it. So now you deal with it!" He left the office slamming the door behind him.

Joan stared apathetically at her daughter. She was irritated that Megan was complaining. *'Did Megan have any idea what it took to talk Tom into coming to meet her? All of the conversations they had to pique his curiosity about her? He's a physician for crying out loud! What the hell is she complaining about?'* "What do you want me to do Megan?"

"Mama, Go to Administration or Human Resources or whoever deals with this kind of problem. Make a report and then we could go to the police."

"Are you crazy? Do you think that I am going to jeopardize my hard earned position for your domestic squabbles? I walked into this building as a maid cleaning dirty toilets and now I am in control. I practically run this place. Are you mad? You are a woman now and part of being a woman is dealing with your problems quietly. He is a good man. Do you think that your father is a piece of pie?"

"Mama, Dad doesn't beat you."

Joan narrowed her eyes at Megan and then she said with a pointed finger. "First of all, your father is weak. He has no ambition. He is scared as hell. He wouldn't even think of it. Tom is a powerful man. He is nothing like your father. "

"So you think I should take it and shut up."

"All I am telling you is to take care of your business quietly and leave us out of it. Our jobs are at stake here. You asked for my advice and here it is. Once you settle down things will change but try not to aggravate the man."

Megan went home and that evening while arranging the place settings at the dinner table Tom picked up a kitchen knife and he held it up as if testing it's sharpness on his finger and then he said casually, "I had lunch with Joan today."

Megan tensed up. What did her mother tell him?

He came closer and grabbed her from behind and he kissed her on the neck. He placed the knife on her throat. "If you ever try to leave me, I'll slit your throat." He kissed her by her ear and then he let her go. "Dinner smells good. Let's eat. I'm hungry." He sat down and began to serve himself from the dishes that were placed on the table.

Chapter 9

The months that passed were horrific for Megan and the visible bruises on her face and arms seemed to go unnoticed by her parents. Joan continued to have a great relationship with Tom. He and Megan frequently went to dinner at her parents' home and her parents came quite often to dinner at the apartment she and Tom shared. Tom forbade Megan to work outside of the home. Her primary job was to take care of him and he isolated her from her friends and family.

A year of horrendous abuse had passed. Those beautiful eyes that once sparkled now hid the secret chamber that housed controlled bitterness and rage she guarded so well. Tom planned a big celebration for their first wedding anniversary at one of the best restaurants in town. Reservations had to be made at least a month in advance.

"Megan, who do you want to invite to our first anniversary dinner?"

"No one, really."

"Come on honey, you must want someone other than your parents?"

"Well, it would be nice to see my grandparents and my Aunt Marcia. I haven't seen them since our wedding."

"Done. You can call and invite them and I'll make the reservations."

She would have liked to see her friends but she didn't want to start a fight so she kept quiet.

———◦⦾◦———

Megan was at her happiest when she was involved in filming and creating beautiful stories with her camera. What was going to be her career had now become her hobby. It was a glorious day, two days before her wedding anniversary and Megan was happy. She got engrossed while filming and lost track of time. Tom had a great day at work. He was his usual charming self to everyone at the hospital. Megan heard the key turn in the door and she knew that it was Tom.

"Hi honey, I am sorry but I got caught up in filming and dinner is running late."

He said nothing but had a quiet calm about him, she handed him a beer. She was a good, quick cook, and dinner was served shortly. After dinner she took her shower and stayed naked. Knowing that she was never allowed to get dressed for bed. Those were her husband's orders. She kissed him goodnight and went to bed. Tom stayed up to watch the eleven o'clock news.

While Megan was in a deep sleep Tom walked into the bedroom quietly while holding a stick. Suddenly, Megan felt a hot painful impact to her head and blood began to flow down her face. The sudden blow to her head left her stunned, although she was instantly awake it took a moment for her to figure out what was happening. "Tom, why? What did I do? Tom please don't hurt me!"

When he saw that she was fully awake he pulled the sheets off of her naked body and began to punch her in the face.

"Tom stop! You can't do this! Stop!" The warm blood ran down her face and onto the sheets, but he didn't seem to care.

"What did you just say? I can't do what? I can do anything I want to do to you." He held both of her feet and tried to drag her out of the bed, but she held on to the bedpost for dear life, he pulled with both hands and all of his strength trying to get her onto the floor but she held on. She wriggled her body and kicking wildly she tried to free her feet and that made him raving mad. "Oh you're resisting me? Who has been filling your head with crap? Do you think you can stop me?"

She knew that if he got her onto the floor that he would kick her. He was fully dressed and his shoe was made of very hard leather. "Tom please don't do this, I beg you please don't."

He finally pried her loose breaking off her fingernails in the process. He dragged and dropped her on the bare hardwood floor and began to kick her, until she was unconscious. Tom was always prepared to mend Megan's cuts and take care of her bruises keeping her away from the emergency room at the hospital. He went to his bag, got his staple gun and he cleaned her head wound with iodine and stapled it. He put smelling salts under her nose to bring her around. When Megan came to, he said to her, "Clean this mess up and clean yourself up."

He walked out of the room and slammed the door behind him. A woozy Megan lay naked and bloody on the floor in a daze.

The night of their anniversary party arrived and Megan got dressed. It was becoming impossible to hide her bruises with makeup. Tom reminded her to wear the diamond and ruby earrings he gave her for their anniversary. She picked up the earrings from among all the marvelous gifts he had given to her over the past year. Every piece of jewelry was significant. Tom spared no expense after a beating. He bought her the best and finest to show his undying love for her and to say how sorry he was. She arrived at the restaurant visibly bruised and wearied. The beatings were taking their toll on her. Her grandparents and her Aunt Marcia were horrified to see their little Megan. Joan took Tom aside and whispered. "Tom, you need to ease up. She looks horrible."

"Joan, you know that I love you but you need to stay out of my business."

"All I am saying is that people are going to begin to talk."

He spoke quietly and deliberately, "I don't give a damn what people think."

Megan's grandparents stared at her throughout the entire meal. They were obviously very upset and refused to speak to Tom. After dinner Tom asked for the bill and Peter Sr. said to the waiter. "Separate bills please. I don't want this bastard paying for anything for me or my family."

Tom paid his part of the bill and he grabbed Megan's hand. "Let's go."

Joan was furious with her father-in-law. "See what you did? You made him mad."

Peter Sr. was livid and spoke sternly to his son. "Son, what are you doing about that situation?"

"Dad, Joan is the one you need to talk to."

"Man, grow some balls! You let her control everything and that little girl always suffers. Rose, let's get out of here before I really lose my temper."

After her in-laws left, Joan attacked Peter verbally. "Why the hell didn't you say something to your father, Peter?"

"Oh, now you want me to say something. You seem to handle things very well all by yourself. You don't *need* me! You sent our daughter to the slaughterhouse and as you can see, it's only a matter of time before we bury her. I hope you are ready for that. But then again, knowing you, you would probably find a nice plot in a white cemetery for her."

"All I have tried to do is give her a good life! I tried to find the best man I could for her so that she could have a good life. Tom is a good man! He is a physician. Half of the women in the hospital would give their right arm to be his wife."

Peter was stunned by his wife's rebuttal. "You are amazing! I can't figure out how your mind works and I'm not even going to try. I'm going home. You are not riding with me. Call yourself a taxi." He left his wife sitting there. On his way home he realized that he needed to warn his daughter. The next day he called Megan. "Hello Megan,"

"Hi Daddy."

"Are you alright?"

The question surprised her. Her father usually avoided any conflict or confrontation that was around him. "Megan, he is going to kill you."

There was just silence.

"Don't say I didn't warn you."

"Daddy?"

"Yes"

"Why do you stay with her? Why do you let her get away with the things she does?"

"I don't like her Megan, but I love her. I can't help the way I feel." He hung up.

Chapter 10

Tom and his friends spent a lot of time at the apartment watching the games on television and drinking. He often insulted his wife in their presence. He missed no opportunity to degrade and humiliate her. Tom, Mike, and the others were watching the game when a commercial came on about weight control products and Tom said to his friends. "If that bitch of mine ever got fat that would be the end."

He was unaware that she was in the adjoining room and heard what he said. Megan remembered an incident in Hawaii. She and Tom were in a restaurant and a family who were all obese came in to eat. Tom said out loud. "Everybody had better order before they eat because when they get through nothing will be left. They should charge them double." Megan was embarrassed and she apologized for his behavior. He said to her, "Don't ever apologize for me. Let's go." He paid the bill and they left.

There was another incident with a young man who walked down the street eating an ice cream cone and Tom walked up to him and said' "Do you really need that? Why do fat people always eat fattening foods? Why can't you control your appetite? Obesity makes you look sloppy." Whenever they encountered overweight people Megan walked away or busied herself.

The months were slowly going by and they were approaching their second wedding anniversary. Megan was pregnant and she was happy. Although when she told Tom that she was pregnant he didn't seem happy. She hoped that having the baby would change Tom's behavior towards her. She imagined Tom playing with their son and the three of them as a loving family. Weight was a big issue with Tom. She had to eat healthy and take care of herself making sure that her only weight gain was the baby's weight.

For a moment she forgot about the abuse and spoke her mind freely. "Tom in two weeks we will be celebrating our second anniversary and I would like to have a few friends over."

"Friends? What friends? You don't have any friends."

"Come on Tom. I want to tell them about the baby. Since the wedding I haven't seen any of my friends. I don't talk to them or go anywhere. The only time I go out is with you."

He got up and he threw her against the wall. "You want to go out? Where do you want to go? You have somewhere you want to go?" She was down on the floor. He kicked her in her back and in her stomach. "Eh! Why don't you tell me? Tell me where you want to go." He kicked and beat her until she couldn't move. She began hemorrhaging. He panicked and he called Joan. "Joan she's bleeding. I think she is going to bleed to death."

"God Tom, you have got to ease up. Call the ambulance."

"I can't do that. I'll lose my license. I don't know what to do. Joan, It's this rage that comes over me. I can't control it. You've got to help me.

"God Tom, let me think." She paced back and forth trying to come up with a solution. "Okay, put her in the car and bring her over here and I'll think of something."

"Thanks Joan. We are on our way."

He stuck a few towels between Megan legs and he lifted her down the stairwell and out the side door of the apartment building. He wanted to avoid the doorman at the front entrance of the apartment building. He took her to his car and drove to Joan's house. While she waited, Joan messed up the house to stage a break-in and told Peter to leave.

"Where am I going to go? It's ten o'clock."

"Do I have to think of everything? I don't care where you go. Go to a bar somewhere. Just get out of here."

Peter left and Tom arrived. He carried his wife into her mother's house and placed her where Joan told him to and he left. Joan called the ambulance and the police.

Two officers and the ambulance arrived at the same time. "Mrs. Garrison, what happened here?"

"I don't know. Apparently she interrupted an intruder. Officer I have to go with my daughter. You can reach me at the hospital."

"Mrs. Garrison, we have to collect evidence from the scene and then we'll meet you over there. Is there anyone here?"

"No. My husband is out. I just came in myself and saw her lying there. I have to call her husband. I don't know how I'll tell him about this. " She left with the ambulance. She wanted to be there when Megan came around. She wanted to warn Megan to tell the same story.

Tom got to the hospital while the cops were still questioning Joan. Megan was too sick to be questioned.

"Mrs. Garrison, we checked the broken window next to the back door. We think this is where he got in but we can't find any fingerprints except for those of you and your husband. There is no evidence of an intruder. Unless your daughter can identify her assailant, we may not be able to solve this case but we will try our best."

Aware that he was being observed by the two police officers, Tom stood by the front desk and acted shocked and surprised. "My God Joan, what happened?"

"Tom, I don't know. I found her on the floor and I called 911 right away." She looked in the direction of the officers but Tom ignored their presence.

He spoke to the nurse. "I want to see my wife."

"Sure Dr. Brinkley. She is in intensive care." Tom went straight to the intensive care unit and stayed by Megan's side to make sure that no one had access to her.

The next day Marcia brought Rose to see her granddaughter and she was angry. She kept her back to Tom. "Hi honey, how are you doing?"

"Fine."

"Fine? Why are you allowing this bastard to do this to you?" She raised her hand as if to stop Megan from lying. "Don't even say a word. He did this to you and no one on this God's great earth will ever convince me differently."

Marcia sat with a wet towel wiping Megan head with cold water. The tears flowed in silence.

Rose continued. "That mother of yours will rot in hell! I don't know what motivates her to do the things she does. Why would she lie for this animal?"

Megan was scared. She did not want Tom to get angry, he would only take it out on her. The only protection she had was being in the hospital and if he had her released she would be in real trouble. "Grandma, I don't know what you are talking about. Mama is telling the truth."

"Okay. If you want to stick to that story then there is nothing that I can do. I have to go. Take care of yourself my child. I'll be praying for you." She looked Tom dead in the eye. "You are evil in its purest form. I hate you and wish that you would drop dead. Dead, I tell you! Marcia let's get out of here before *I* commit murder." Rose was a very religious woman but that day she would have made a pact with the Devil if he would get rid of Tom.

Megan was better in a few days and was moved to a regular room. Tom needed to get out of that room. He left Megan alone and went to get something to eat

Chapter 11

"Hello sleepyhead."
Megan lay back and the tears ran down the side of her face. She was glad to see her friends. That gentle voice was Ariel's and next to her was Lulu, Lizzie and Jennifer. She hadn't accepted their phone calls or seen them since the wedding. They stood around her bed.

"How are you doing?"

"How did you know?"

Lizzie put her finger to her lips. "Shhh. Don't talk. The neighborhood is buzzing with the news. You know that nothing ever happens there and now this."

She could see in their eyes that they knew. They were all crying and Lizzie squeezed Lulu's hand. She warned him to keep his cool and not voice his opinion, but he couldn't help it. "Honey, he is gonna kill you. We don't believe that story your mother is telling. It's appalling the way she protects him."

"Lulu, how did you all find out?"

"Your grandmother called us. She thought that you needed your friends. She said that she can't reach you and she was hoping that we could talk some sense into you. By the way, where is the devil?"

Megan smiled but her face hurt. "He went to lunch but please don't make any trouble when he returns. I don't want to make him angry."

They all held her hands and Lizzie said, "You poor thing. Let's change the subject. We brought you some magazines and a book for you to read. Don't rush to get out of here. You are protected as long as you are here."

Megan smiled and said, "So tell me what has been going on with you guys. I really miss you." They brought her up to date with everything that was happening in their lives and then she apologized properly to Jennifer. "Jen, I am sorry for saying that you were jealous of me and Tom. I was a fool. I am so sorry."

Jennifer with a wave of her hand said, "Don't worry. We understand why you needed to stay away. We said those things about Tom because we wanted to save you from situations like this. If you waited you would have found out what kind of a person he was. He rushed you into marriage because he was afraid that if you got to know him, you wouldn't marry him."

"You can't tell anyone he beat me. Please promise."

Lulu was stunned. "Tell anyone? Baby, your bruises speak for themselves!"

Lizzie looked at Lulu and silently begged him to just agree to keep quiet. He smiled and they all said, "We promise." They all promised to keep silent. Ariel spoke through trembling lips. "Don't worry, we'll always be here for you." They decided to leave before Tom returned from lunch.

Down in the hospital cafeteria Tom got his lunch.
"Tom! Over here."

His college buddy called out to him. Tom walked over to Mike's table and sat down with his food and soda.

"I've been busy since Megan got hurt. How are the guys?"

Mike was uneasy but he felt that he had to talk to Tom. Someone had to.

"Tom you got to stop. I like Megan. She is a nice girl and she loves you. Why do you have to hurt her like that?"

Tom looked around and was well aware that his colleagues were close enough to overhear their conversation if they got loud. So he said quietly, "What are you talking about? Didn't you hear? She walked in on some robber in her parents' home and he beat her up."

"Tom! It's me! We went to college together. I know you. You almost killed that girl, what was her name? I think it was Susan. You remember? I helped you dump her over in that deserted alley because you wanted it to look like someone robbed her. You almost killed her. Tom, you got to stop or you'll end up in prison. You're going to kill Megan."

Tom gritted his teeth. "Keep your voice down. Do you think that you're better than me?" Tom scowled and continued speaking in a quiet but threatening tone "Don't forget who got you this job. You work here because of me. I have always had your back. Are you turning on me now?" Tom stood up. He smiled for his audience. He turned back to face Mike and he grimaced at Mike and under his breath he said. "Keep out of my business."

"Like I said Tom, you are going to end up in prison as somebody's bitch and you will be deserving of every minute of it."

Tom tightened his fist. He looked around still smiling and decided to walk away. He went back up to Megan's room. Her friends had already left and she saw no reason to mention that they were there. She pretended to be asleep but Tom angrily woke her up. "When are you going to get out of this place? I can't take another day sitting here babysitting you."

Megan kept quiet. She saw his controlled rage and she wanted no part of it. A nurse who liked Megan and highly respected Tom walked into the room. "Doctor, you look tired. I can sit with your wife for a while so that you can get some fresh air. I can see that you are very protective of her but no one will be able to hurt her here. No one will think any less of you if you decided to go back to work."

Trying to impress his nurse he looked at Megan and said. "I would like to go back to work."

"Megan said, "Go.""

"Are you sure, honey?"

"I'm sure."

Tom leaned over, kissed Megan, and whispered, "You'd better watch what you say. Then he said out loud, "I love you honey, feel better." He then turned to the nurse and said, "Mary, Thank you. I was getting cabin fever."

"You are welcome Doctor." Mary smiled at Megan. "You'll be just fine. Is there anything I can get for you?"

"No, thank you. I am fine."

"I'll just sit here to ease your husband's mind. He is very worried about you. It's hard to lose a baby but you are young. You'll have many more."

Megan smiled. Nothing could make her feel better. She had lost her baby. Someone she could love with her whole heart and who would love her unconditionally.

Megan recovered from four broken ribs but the loss of her baby would take time to heal. She had enough of Tom's abuse.

How will she be able to escape this marriage? When she returned from Hawaii she installed cameras around the apartment to document the abuse. She replaced the full tapes with new tapes weekly and she stored those tapes in a private hiding place at her parents' home. She knew that Tom would kill her if he found them. She had to come up with a plan.

She read many stories of women who were murdered, maimed, one who was drenched with gasoline and burned. The papers said that her skin melted like wax. Tom had left that article for her to see. From the beginning, she knew she would not leave this marriage and live to tell. He had to leave. It had to be his idea. But how, how could she get him to walk out of her life for good?

Chapter 12

Megan racked her brains to come up with a plan of escape. Her grandmother had told Megan about Jesus as a little girl and Megan became a Christian. Megan, Aunt Marcia, and her grandparents went to church on Sundays while Joan and Peter were at work. After Megan left for college she strayed away but now felt the need to go back to her religious roots. She began to read her bible and she prayed daily.

Megan decided that she was going to take a chance and step out in faith. She began to eat anything and everything she could get her hands on. She baked several cakes and she stuffed herself until she vomited but she kept on eating ice cream, cookies, cakes, bread, peanut butter, and cheese. Every fattening thing she could find she would eat. Three months later her weight gain became visible, when she had gained fifty pounds Tom had enough.

It was a beautiful Thursday morning and Tom had the day off. He usually slept in on his day off but he got up early. Tom walked into the dining room where Megan was eating her breakfast. She jumped up immediately. "Good Morning honey. Let me fix you something to eat. What would you like?"

"I would like to stop you from stuffing your face like a damn pig."

She cowered in preparation for the punches to begin. Beads of perspiration emerged on her forehead and her body shook with fear.

'Look at yourself." He dragged her by her hair to the mirror in the hallway. "Take a good look in the mirror, you are a big fat pig." He pushed her down on the ground took out his penis and urinated in her face. "That's what pigs get. Do you know why I married you? I married you because no one else wanted you. Your mother practically begged me to take you. You are nothing but a waste of time."

He lifted his hand in an attempt to strike her but something in her stood up. She suddenly felt strong. The fear left and the facial expression he was used to seeing changed. She didn't look afraid any more, she didn't cry or begged, she rose up from within, that private rage was unleashed and she spoke courageously,

"Go ahead, kill me! Death is better than living with you! I don't care anymore. Just get it over with. I just don't care anymore!"

He raised his hand to hit her but his hand was frozen in mid air, it was as if he was being restrained by a powerful force greater than he. He moved away from her, it was sudden and strange. He turned and walked away from her. Megan pulled herself up from the ground, soaked in urine. She made it into the shower and stripped naked. She turned on the warm water and she sat on the shower floor in the fetal position. The warm water was in full flow on her entire body.

She cried out loud. Tears flowed from the depths of her bowels as she cried. "God, I don't deserve this! I DON'T deserve this at all. I prayed and I asked You to send someone to LOVE me. TO JUST LOVE ME! That's all I wanted. And this is what I get!? It's not right! It's just not right! It hurts! My heart hurts! It really hurts. I am a good person. I really am and I don't deserve this. I feel sooo helpless! I have suffered the same abuse over and over, I don't even get time to heal from one assault before another one occurs. He hurts me over and over again and no one does anything about it. I feel like I'm in a deep hole and I can't get out. I am so desperate and I need help!" She continued to sob out loud until she was exhausted and then she finished showering and got dressed.

Chapter 13

Megan prepared Tom's lunch that day and he ate in silence. That evening he moved into the guest room. He couldn't stand to look at or talk to her but he didn't leave. Weeks had passed and she became discouraged. She prayed and prayed but he stayed in the apartment. The beatings had stopped, the sex stopped, but he stayed on.

Megan decided to call on her friends for help. She dialed Ariel's cell. The phone rang, "Hi Ariel, this is Megan."

"Hi Megan, how are you doing?" Ariel was a reporter at WJLB Television Station and she was happily married.

"Ariel, I want to leave Tom and I need your help."

"Sure Megan. What do you want me to do?"

"I called Jen and Lizzie and we are going to meet at Lulu's. Can you meet us there? Ariel, I am desperate."

"Sure honey, I'll be there."

━━━◈━━━

They all met at Lulu's. Lizzie was a successful fashion designer. She was a full figured gal who was always put together perfectly. Her dyed bright red hair was always fashionable. She was shocked to see how Megan was dressed. Lizzie reached out and touched

Megan. She scrutinized her outfit and then she said, "Megan, missionaries dress more appealing than you do. You have gained some weight but overweight women are dressing sexy these days. I'll have to hook you up girl, you look horrible." Fashion was always on Lizzie's mind. If she had her way she would dress the entire world.

Megan ignored Lizzie's criticism and walked pass her into the living room. She headed straight for the television and DVD player. She was anxious to show them the DVD she held in her hand. She had piqued the curiosity of the entire group. Megan in a quiet and grave voice said, "Look, I really need you to see this." The DVD of the abuse she suffered was much more than any of them could have imagined. During a particular scene, a very pregnant Megan was being repeatedly kicked in the stomach by Tom. As she began to hemorrhage, Ariel covered her mouth with her hand and ran out from the room in horror. Lulu leaped from the couch and turned the DVD off. With tears streaming down his face he said, "I just can't watch anymore!" He embraced Megan with all the love he could muster and it moved her to tears. Still in his embrace he rocked her gently from side to side and he said, "Megan I love you. Don't worry, we're going to save you from that bastard."

Lizzie was still in a daze. She stared at the blank television screen. She mumbled to herself, "If I had not seen this DVD with my own eyes I wouldn't have believed it. Her tears began to flow freely and she was barely able to speak. She said, My God Megan, you have been through hell. We'll help you."

A tearful Meagan walked over to where Lizzie was sitting and wiping her eyes she said, "You know, I've often wondered if God is all seeing and all knowing why didn't He stop me from marrying Tom?"

Lizzie answered her promptly. "Honey he tried. Do you remember that night at the restaurant when we questioned the urgency of the marriage? Maybe it was his way of bringing to your attention that you were about to make a mistake. My mother always said that God is a gentleman, He doesn't bombard us. He gently nudges us, and most of the time we don't want to hear what He has to say. But when we have to suffer the consequences of our unwise decisions, we blame Him."

Lulu noticed that Jennifer seemed to be unmoved by what they all just witnessed. He said, "I'd better check on Ariel I can hear her crying." Lulu brought Ariel back to the room and he said, "We're going to fix this. Come on, we need a group hug."

They all came around Megan and had a group hug like they did when they were in grade school.

Lulu took Megan's hand in his and he said. "Just put your little hands into mine and we will get rid of that bastard you're married to. Now let's get to work."

The plan was that Lulu would use his skills as a make-up artist to make Megan look fat. She would increase in size gradually until Tom left. Hopefully Tom would continue to leave her alone because if he insisted on having sex he would find out that Megan was not as fat as she pretended.

Lizzie took over the designing of the suit. "Lulu you need to make the suit shapely. Fat does not have to be square or round. Give her nice full breasts, a waist, hips, and shapely legs. Her face doesn't have to be too fat. Don't add on too much to her face. I am going to design some outfits that would compliment your body Megan. I'll call it *Big & Luscious Designs*.

Chapter 14

Their plan worked. Tom was totally disgusted with his wife's weight gain. She increased in size to approximately 200 lbs when Tom decided he had enough. He emptied the apartment and left her with absolutely nothing. Tom was out of her life and she was happy.

The five of them sat around Lulu's dining table brainstorming Megan's future as a single woman. Megan explained to them, "I don't know what to do. I can't return home or confide in my parents. If I confide in my mother Tom will find out and the situation will turn out worse than I could ever imagine."

The apartment where Tom and Megan lived was luxurious and expensive. She couldn't afford to keep it. Megan crossed her hands in her lap. Her head was bowed in defeat. She was worried. "I have bills to pay and I need to find a place to live. I have to find a job while I wait for my divorce."

Lizzie said, "I think that your job should be a low key position, something to keep you hidden. You can't let him get a hint that you are pretending."

"I know. I will wear this body suit and continue to pretend for as long as I have to. I can't let him know that I want the divorce or he won't give it to me. It has to be his idea."

They were all trying to think how to help their friend. Jennifer secretly believed that Megan deserved her plight. She felt that Megan was privileged and spoiled. Jennifer was jealous and always compared her life to Megan's. She didn't want to, but felt pressured to help Megan because Lizzie, Lulu and Ariel were doing their best to help their friend. She had to be seen contributing something. Jennifer worked for one of the biggest law firms in America. It was a family practice of corporate attorneys. She didn't want Megan working with her in the office, but felt that the job she was about to offer suited Megan.

Jennifer said, "Megan, my boss is having personal problems. His wife is bipolar and he's looking for someone to take care of his home and kids." She proudly said, "As his executive assistant, I can hire you."

"I'll take it."

"I believe that you will love working for him, everyone at the Firm does. We are like a great big family. He's rich and powerful but he's real cool. Although he's the boss he's on first name basis with everyone and he's a good Christian man. I have to warn you though, you have to attend church on Sundays with him and his family."

Attending church would not be a problem for Megan. "I'll take it. I'll take it."

"I will make the arrangements right away for your interview with him" Jennifer got on the phone to her boss.

Lulu was in deep thought trying to figure out the entire plan Megan needed.

"Megan, you can give up the apartment and move in with me."

"Lulu, I can't do that?"

"Yes honey, you can. That way I can keep an eye on you."

Megan hugged Lulu. "I love you."

Lulu continued, "You'll be at work most of the time anyway. I won't take no for an answer. Now let's see what else you need to do. Don't use your cell phone, get a disposable cell phone, and cash your checks at the check-cashing store. Use cash for everything, and if you need a credit card get a prepaid one. You have to let that bastard think that you are lost without him."

Chapter 15

Jennifer and Megan left immediately for the interview with her boss. They drove up the circular driveway and up to the mansion. Jennifer rang the doorbell and to Megan's surprise, a tall, slim, very handsome and naturally tanned man answered the doorbell. His facial features were as that of a magnificent sculpture, and power exuded his physical make-up. *Wow! He's handsome!* Megan thought. *Why did I think that he was white?*

"Hello, Jennifer"

"Hi Jackson, this is Megan, my friend." She turned to Megan and said, "Megan, this is Mr. Jackson Montgomery."

With an outstretched hand he said, "Hello Megan, I'm Jackson. Come on in." His touch was electrifying, Megan cautioned herself, *this is going to be my boss and he is married, besides, the last thing I need is to complicate my life.*

"Let's go into my office." He held a coffee mug in his hand while they walked to his home office. He sat at the edge of his desk and offered them the two available seats.

"May I offer you a cup of coffee?"

They both said, "No thank you."

He set his cup down on the desk and began to speak. "I'm sure that Jennifer told you that I need someone to manage our home. It's no secret that my wife is bipolar. When she takes her meds she's okay and when she doesn't, it's hell in this house. I need a very strong person. When I say strong I mean emotionally, more so than physically. This job can be very draining and Jennifer seems confident that you can handle it." He looked at both of them and waited for a response. When none came he continued. "So you can go ahead and give it a try. If you have any problems please don't hesitate to call me at work or wherever I may be. My family comes first at all times. Any questions?"

"No Mr. Montgomery, not right now but I am sure that I will have some later."

"Well, if you want the job it's yours and call me Jackson."

"Thank you. I accept, Jackson"

Jackson smiled and extended his hand to Megan. "Welcome to the family." He liked her. She carried herself elegantly and her smile made him feel warm inside. He got up. "Let me introduce you to my family and show you around." He led the way upstairs to a beautiful suite where his wife was. Michelle Montgomery was a beautiful and delicate blonde. She seemed sweet and shy. " Megan this is my wife. Michelle, this is Megan. Megan is going to take care of things around here from now on so that Mom could have some time to herself. Michelle smiled and shook Megan's hand. She said, "Welcome to the crazy house. I'm the crazy lady."

Jackson said, "As you can see my wife has a weird sense of humor." His mother sat opposite Michelle. Mrs. Montgomery Sr. was a very petite brunette. Her smile was kind and she spoke in a gentle manner. She extended her hand to Megan, "Welcome dear. I hope that you'll be happy here." But she eyed Megan's oversized body.

Megan felt self-conscious. "Thank you Ma'am, I'm sure I'll be, she replied.

Jennifer was quietly speaking to Michelle and then she said, "Hello Mrs. Montgomery. How are you doing?"

"I am doing fine Jennifer. It's good to see you."

Jackson said, "Now let me introduce you to our three beautiful angels. They're down in the great room watching television."

His mother said immediately, "I sure hope not. They're supposed to be doing their homework and watching their brother. Megan you're going to have to be very stern with those girls."

Jackson smiled and said to Megan. "Don't worry with Mom. They're really nice kids. They have a lot to deal with." Megan and Jennifer followed him into the great room and there on the floor in front of the television were ten-year-old blonde Christine, the splitting image of her mother, eight-year-old Sarah, the splitting image of her grandmother and little three-year-old Jacob who had the beautiful brown tanned skin like his father and a beautiful head of curly hair. "Kids this is Megan. You have to listen to her. She is going to be running things around here from now on."

Christine wined, "What about Grandma? She takes care of us."

"Grandma is tired and needs a rest. You'll still see her often but Megan is going to be here everyday and she is going to take care of you." He picked up Jacob while he spoke. "I want you to promise me that you will listen to Megan and be good. Okay?"

They all said, "Okay."

Megan bent over and shook the children's hands and she said, "It's nice to meet you. I hope we can be friends. Are you guys watching *The Electric Company*? That used to be my favorite show."

Christine said, "Really! Who is your favorite character?"

Megan said, "Manny."

And Sarah said, "Me too! Me too!"

Christine said, "Jacob dances to all the music."

A shy Jacob buried his head in his father's chest.

Megan loved children and had easily bonded with these kids.

"Would you like to watch it with us?" Said Sarah.

"I'd love to watch it with you." Megan looked at Jennifer who eagerly said," Go right ahead I'll wait for you. I need to discuss a few things with Jackson anyway. Jackson smiled and he and Jennifer left the room. After the show Megan got up to leave. Jacob ran to her and put his little arms around her leg. He asked, "Do you have to leave?"

Megan said, I promise I'll be back as soon as I can pack my things. She held Jacob's hand as she walked over to where Jackson and Jennifer were talking. She said, "Excuse me Jackson."

He turned to listen to what she was saying and he picked up Jacob. "I see the little tike here really likes you, Megan."

Jacob bent his head shyly and Megan said, "I like you too, Jacob. I'm going home to pack and I'll be back first thing tomorrow morning."

Jackson said, "Good. That would be a great help. I'll introduce you to the staff you will be supervising then." He walked her and Jennifer to the door. When they got into the car Megan said, "You didn't tell me that he was black."

"I don't think of him that way. I don't think anyone who knows him does. He and his father have transcended racial barriers. Their practice is one of the largest in the country. They're really brilliant men but they like white women. You saw their wives."

Megan was excited about the job. "Jen, thank you for all your help. I like this family and I know that I'm going to like working with them."

"You're welcome."

Megan reported for duty the next day as planned and Jackson called the other employees to meet her. First there was Penny Gibson. "Penny keeps an eye on Michelle so that Mom can run errands and manage the estate. Penny Gibson this is Megan Brinkley. She is going to manage things around here." Penny gave a half hearted greeting to Megan. "Hi."

Megan ignored her rudeness and greeted her cheerfully "Penny, It's nice to meet you."

Jackson continued his tour. "Let's step outside. I want you to meet Grant he keeps the grounds and makes sure that everything around here is working. He has three helpers but you will manage the entire staff including Grant." Just then Grant came walking up to the house. "Good morning Sir."

"Good morning Grant. This is Megan Brinkley. She is the one you will speak to when you need supplies. She is our new manager."

Grant with a charming smile took off his hat and bowed. "Welcome."

Megan said, "Thank you."

Jackson smiled and with a gentle hand steered Megan back inside. "You'll meet the others later. We also have a staff of cleaners that come once a week. The housekeeping you have to do is light and some cooking is involved. Well, have a good day I have to be at the office right about now."

"Have a good day Jackson." Megan was excited to begin her new job.

Chapter 16

Megan didn't tell her family that she was employed. She had to keep up the façade that she was suffering. Dressed in one of her ugly shift dresses, Megan went to her parents for dinner that Friday evening. Joan, in an attempt to reunite Tom and Megan, invited Tom to dinner. Tom refused to look at Megan. After the main course Megan had three helpings of desert. Disgusted, Joan could not contain her anger. "How the hell did you get so fat? I raised you to eat healthy."

"Mama, I'm trying but I can't help myself. I eat when I'm upset or nervous."

Joan said under her breath." I guess that's all the damn time."

Megan pretended that she didn't hear what her mother said. "Mama I don't know what to do. How am I going to survive?" She turned to talk to Tom but he kept his head down. His disgust was evident. "Tom, I don't have anywhere to go. I'm your wife." She stuffed her face with another helping. She was really hungry. She starved herself the entire week to give this performance. "Tom, what am I going to do?"

Tom answered abruptly. "I don't know and I really don't care. We're through."

Joan asked, "What do you expect him to do Megan? You've got to help yourself and maybe after you lose some of that weight Tom might see it in his heart to take you back."

Peter could not believe his ears. His wife was siding with an abuser. A man who would just as soon kill their daughter, if he thought that he could get away with it. Peter knew that the only reason Joan really liked Tom was because he was white. He had never felt such disgust for her as he did this moment. He was also upset with Megan for groveling at the man's feet. Yet he said and did nothing.

Megan explained, "I have interviewed. I have sought employment." She looked desperate and while she was still talking, she took another piece of chocolate cake.

Joan grabbed the cake out of her hand. "Give me that damn cake! You look like a fat hog!"

Megan got up from the table, obviously upset. "Mama would you like me to help with the dishes?"

It was all Joan could do but slap the crap out of Megan. "No! Your father will stack the damn dishes in the dishwasher!"

"Well then I'll say goodnight." And with that she left.

Tom and Joan talked while Peter stacked the dishwasher. "Tom, I don't know what to say, how did she get so big? What happened?"

"I tried Joan, but I can't handle it any longer. I hope that you and I could still be friends. You mean a great deal to me."

Joan was glad to hear him say that. "Tom I feel privileged to be your friend."

Well, I'll see you at the hospital tomorrow." Joan walked him out. On her way back she bumped into Peter who stared her down. He said under his breath, "I guess no one has to ask you whose side you're on."

Joan sighed and shook her head. "It's no use talking to you?" She continued walking to her room.

———◦《◦》◦———

Megan went straight to Lulu's apartment. Her friends were waiting patiently to hear all about her family dinner. She walked into Lulu's apartment and she began to laugh. She laughed so heartily and couldn't stop.

"Honey, when you finish tickling yourself we would like to hear all about it."

"I should get an Oscar. I begged and I ate. He was so disgusted and my mother was her usual charming self."

Lulu cautioned her. "Don't get too cocky, Baby girl. This man can destroy you. I don't know why he is waiting but be careful. I know that you have already begun to lose the weight but you have to continue to wear that suit and make-up from the moment you get up until you go to bed. You don't want to be surprised with an unannounced visit from Tom. Be prepared."

She hugged Lulu and her friends. "I know Lulu but just let me enjoy this moment."

"Honey you can't afford to enjoy anything until that man is out of your life and you are far away from this place."

"I know. I know. I'll wait and when the divorce is over, I'll become so broken up that I will have to go far away from this place to recover and I will never return."

———◦《◦》◦———

Megan spoke to her parents once in a while but she spoke to her grandmother daily. With daily exercise and a very good diet she lost the weight and was back to her original size six but faithfully wore her fat suit. Lizzie kept her word and Megan had become her fashionable and sexy overweight model. With Lulu's help Megan's make-up was always perfectly applied. Time went by quickly. Three months had passed and no divorce.

Chapter 17

Megan loved her new job. She got up at 5 a.m. promptly, had morning devotion, got dressed, and went downstairs to begin her daily schedule. Jackson liked her. She fit well into his family. Michelle tried her best to be good and stay on her meds. Megan sat down to talk with Penny about Michelle.

"Penny I need you to check Mrs. Montgomery's medicine and make sure that she swallows the tablets. I made this schedule that I want you to follow and I would appreciate it if you would report any strange behavior you might observe during your time with Mrs. Montgomery."

"Who do you think you're talking to? I've been working for this family for years and I don't need you coming in here telling me what to do! I've watched Michelle in and out of her spells for years. Don't tell me what to do!"

"Penny, I was hoping that we could get along but whether you like it or not, I am your boss."

Penny shrugged and walked out of the room. She refused to take orders from Megan and continued to do as she pleased. Megan realized that Penny's termination was inevitable and it occurred that very week.

Penny had finished working for the day and Megan called out to her while she was leaving. "Penny"

"*What?*"

"May I see you for a minute?"

"Whatever it is you want, will have to wait until tomorrow. I'm off the clock."

"I really need to see you now."

Penny stood at the door of Jackson's office and sighed loudly. "What do you want?"

"Penny, it's not working out for us. I'm going to have to let you go."

Penny shook her head. "I knew this was coming. The day I met you I knew that you were trouble. Give a black person a little power and it goes to their head. Bye. When you woke up this morning you knew that you were gonna fire me. Why didn't you just fire me over the phone? You would've saved me the trouble of having to see your fat ass."

Megan wasn't going to entertain any more rudeness from Penny. "Goodbye Penny, I'll mail you your check."

The children however were well mannered and very protective towards each other. Grant tried to charm Megan every chance he got. He would bring her roses from the garden. He promptly repaired whatever she told him needed his attention. He kept forgetting to submit bills and kept lousy records for money spent. With a charming smile he'd say, "I've got that bill somewhere." Or, "I forgot. I'll get the paper work to you later." He could never produce a detail account of the money he spent. Her inner gut told her to keep a stern eye on him.

It was a beautiful and bright Wednesday morning, a day like any other day. Megan got dressed and went downstairs to begin her routine. The sight of a dark figure sitting in the corner of the kitchen made her jump. "Jackson, what are you doing up so early and sitting in the dark?"

His head was in both of his hands. He looked like he was in a daze. "She's gone."

"Gone? Who's gone?"

"Michelle left. Here is the note she left." He handed her the note.

Jackson,

I can't do this anymore. Megan is doing a fine job. The children love her. I feel confident that they will be alright. I don't expect anything from you. Just get the divorce and get it over with. I'll be at my parents' home. Please don't try to come or bring the children. I just can't give you all what you need. Jackson you are a good man and deserve a normal life. Please let me go so that you can live your life the way you were meant to. Thank Megan for me she is a good person. See if you can help her to get rid of that son of a bitch she married.

Love,
Michelle

Chapter 18

Megan's heart hurt for him. She wanted to put her arms around him and comfort him but felt that would be inappropriate. "Jackson, I am so sorry."

He asked, "Did you have any idea? Did she say anything to you about this?"

"No. She has been very quiet and normal the only difference is that she has been on the phone quite a lot and every time I enter the room she would hang up. I just thought that she wanted her privacy and I gave her as much as I could but kept my eye on her activities which were normal."

"She had to be planning this. She must have called a cab. The cars are all in the garage. I have to talk to Grant. Maybe he saw something."

"How did you know that she left?"

"I got a call from her father. I thought that something was wrong with my mother-in-law when the phone rang at 4 a.m. and I heard my father-in-law's voice. But he told me Michelle was with them and that she was safe and not to worry. He wants me to comply with her wishes."

"I'm sorry Jackson. What are you going to do?"

"I don't have a choice. I will do what is best for Michelle. You read her letter. She feels burdened. She wants out. I'll have to tell the children the truth. We've always told them the truth. I'm not going to give them any false hope by sugar coating the situation." He looked up at Megan and he looked so adorable. He looked like a little boy in need of comfort. "Megan, they will need you more than they ever did. Can you handle it?"

"Jackson, I'm here for you and the children. I'll do my best to make their lives as normal as possible."

"Thank you Megan. I'm really going to hold you to that."

After Michelle left, it took some time but the household became peaceful and the children adjusted to their new life without their mother. Sundays after church Jackson cooked dinner. He and the children played ball games while Megan watched them from the veranda. She enjoyed the sea breeze and caught up on her reading. At times she took footage of film and they would sit after dinner and laugh at the things they did on her short movies. Jackson played the piano and they all would sing. After the children were safely tucked in, he and Megan would have hot chocolate or a glass of milk before retiring to bed.

Months had gone by and Jackson got his divorce quietly and quickly. He didn't want to admit it but he felt relieved. The normality of his life felt unbelievably good. He looked forward to his morning conferences with Megan; they talked about the children and the household. He told her of the difficulties he encountered during his day at the office, the employees, and about his colleagues. They confided in each other. Her weight was the only secret she kept.

Jackson came out of his home office and walked over to the coffee pot and poured a cup. He thought to himself as he poured his coffee. *This is how a family should be, nice and peaceful.* He looked over to where Megan was packing the dishwasher and he admired her. *She is beautiful. There is that feeling again. She had been hurt badly and has said vehemently that she has sworn off men.* Megan looked up and their eyes met. He smiled, "Coffee?" He asked.

"Yes, thank you. That sounds good." She took the cup of coffee and closed her eyes and smelled it. "It's heavenly."

He smiled. *How can anyone make a cup of coffee look so deliciously good?*

They sat down on the veranda off the kitchen that overlooked the ocean. The ocean breeze blew her hair. Jackson liked Megan's natural curly hair.

"You made a very nice dinner last night."

"Surprised that a man can cook?"

She laughed. "I know men cook. I just don't know any who do."

"I love to cook. It relaxes me."

"Cook away. I'm all for it."

"It's nice having someone to talk to. I used to talk about Michelle and the kids with Jennifer but now I have you."

"How is Jen taking it? She prides herself on being your *Executive Assistant* you know."

Jackson chuckled, "She does, sometimes she can be very demanding and I have to remind her that I am the one in charge. I try to keep a professional relationship with her. She volunteered to help manage the estate before you came. I wasn't comfortable letting her do it but I had no choice. I really needed her help. I am so glad that you came along."

She reminded herself that Jennifer and Jackson were close. He confided in Jennifer but when she got too personal he reminded her that their relationship was a professional one. Megan never wanted him to ever have to remind her that their relationship was that of employer and employee. "Jackson, I'm really glad that I can be of help to you."

He cupped her hands in his. His touch sent a thrill up her spine. She controlled her trembling hand. His eyes pierced hers and in a very soft voice he said, "You are. I couldn't do this without you." He looked at his watch. "I'd better get dressed for work."

After their time together Jackson went to get ready for the office. The phone rang and she went to answer it.

"Hello Lulu."

"Megan, I am calling to confirm our date for tonight."

"I'll be there. Have I ever not shown up?"

"I have a new suit for you and your face mask needs a new touch up. You need to keep this charade going."

"Lulu, Have you heard something?"

"No. But you know how things are. When you least expect the devil, he shows up. Be prepared."

"Okay Daddy, but I serve a great God who promises to deliver me from the devil."

They both laughed and hung up and as if by telepathy, a few minutes later Tom called. He got the number from Joan.

"Hello."

"Megan I need to see you. I'm coming over."

He hung up. Jackson had not left for the office as yet. She called to him.

"Jackson?"

"Yes."

"I need to ask you a favor. My husband wants to see me. He is on his way over here."

Before she could finish speaking he said. "I'll be here. I will sit where I can keep an eye on you at all times. I won't let him touch you. I promise."

"Thank you, Jackson."

Jackson meant it. He was not going to let that bastard hurt one hair on her head. He took out his gun that he had hidden in his safe. He made sure that it was loaded and ready to fire. He would never hurt anyone but he had no idea what frame of mind Tom was in. He had heard of many men who injured or killed their spouses and he wanted to be prepared.

Tom arrived an hour later. Megan was nervous but Jackson's presence comforted her. Tom refused to look at her disgustingly overweight body. He looked everywhere but at Megan when he spoke. "I filed for the divorce citing reasons of desertion. Just sign here."

"Honey, what went wrong? How did we come to this?"

"Don't call me honey. It's over. Sign this and let me go."

She didn't want to over play her hand. He needed to continue thinking that he was the one who needed the divorce. If for one second he caught on to her game, he would stay married just to spite her. She knew him enough to be certain of this. She took the papers and as professionally as she could be, she called her boss over. "Mr. Montgomery, this is Tom, my husband."

Tom corrected her. "Her soon to be ex-husband."

Jackson ignored Tom and he looked directly at Megan. In a gentle voice he said,

"What can I do for you?"

She handed him the divorce papers. Real tears steamed down her cheeks. She cried for the man she thought she had married not this monster that stood before her.

Jackson kept his eyes on Tom. He waited to make sure that she was all right and then he glanced over the papers while still keeping an eye on Tom. "I am not a divorce lawyer but everything seems in order. Is this what you want? If it is, then go ahead and sign it."

Tom took the signed divorce papers and put them into his inside coat pocket. He looked her in the eye this time. A scowl appeared on his face and he spat out, "How did you get so ugly?"

Megan smiled within and thought to herself. *If I didn't make myself ugly as you put it, I'd probably be dead.* "I don't know Tom. I just don't know."

Jackson heard his comment and wondered, *how could he call Megan ugly? Blind fool!*

Tom shrugged his shoulder and said, "Don't call me or try to see me. It's over and I'm moving on with my life. The divorce papers will be delivered in the mail."

Tom extended his hand to Jackson but Jackson ignored it. Jackson walked over to the door and held it open. Tom left, and Jackson put his arms around Megan, and she wept on his shoulder. It felt good to be held like this. His scent was refreshing and she didn't want to let go.

Jackson nuzzled his face against her curly locks. Her hair smelled heavenly. He hadn't held a woman like this a long time and it felt natural and good. He wanted to hold her in his arms forever.

She pulled away and felt that she had to explain her tears. "I'm not crying because I love him. I'm crying because I was such a fool to let him do the things he did to me."

"Thank God that you got out. There are many women who try and fail. Don't beat yourself up. You survived. I'll call in a few favors and get the divorce done quickly." He handed her his handkerchief. "I don't ever want to see sad tears from those eyes again."

"Thank you, Jackson. I really appreciate what you are doing. I can't wait to be free of that monster."

Chapter 19

Megan was overjoyed and that night she and her friends celebrated. They got together at Lulu's loft. His spacious two-bedroom loft was above Lizzie's studio and her office. The loft was ostentiously decorated as only Lulu could have done. Everyone talked loudly and laughed heartily at each other's jokes and was having lots of fun. The Chinese food was good and they had already emptied three bottles of wine.

"So Megan, tell us what happened when Tom came over."

"Well, Lulu, it was like this. He called and I got scared. I didn't know what he wanted and I didn't want to be alone with him. I told Jackson that Tom was coming and he volunteered to stick around and be visible. I was a bit surprised that after signing the papers, I felt sad."

"Why?"

"I don't know how to describe it but I cried for the man I thought I had married. Tom was not him. Jackson is a wonderful man. He let me cry on his shoulder and I felt so much better after."

Lulu eyed Jennifer who immediately said, "It's after twelve and I'm going to head home. Aren't you going? You have to get up bright and early to get the kids off to school and make breakfast for your boss. Don't you?"

"Jen, I'm spending the night with Lulu. I asked Jackson for tomorrow off. He took the kids over to his parents. Why don't you take tomorrow off? Let's have a pajama party. I'm sure that Jackson won't mind."

"I am not his maid, I'm his executive assistant. He needs me to be there because he relies heavily on me."

"Ouch! Girl, did you just get slapped down?"

"Lulu, I think I did." Megan giggled. She was a bit tipsy from all the wine she drank and Jennifer was in no mood to keep this party going.

"Look I'm tired. I'm going home."

Ariel and Lizzie said, "We're right behind you."

After they left, Megan and Lulu got into pajamas and began to gossip and giggle until they eventually fell asleep. The next day was a special day. They shopped and lunched at Megan's favorite restaurant. They were both exhausted that evening when they got home.

Chapter 20

Megan returned to work the next morning. The kids were with their grandmother who volunteered to take the girls to school and keep Jacob for the day. Jackson left for the office and was not expected to return with the children until dinner time. Sarah had the leading role in an upcoming play at school and Jackson planned to take Christine and Jacob to her rehersal that afternoon. Megan rejoiced and sang as she did her chores. She held a large pot spoon as her microphone as she belted out boldly the song "*I Wanna Know What Love Is.*" She was going to be a single lady. Free at last. She knew that this was going to be a great day.

The doorbell rang, Megan looked at the clock. She wasn't expecting anyone. She hurried to the door and opened it. It was the mailman. He delivered a package of developed film. Megan thought to herself, *I didn't send any film to be developed. Maybe this is something I forgot.*

She eagerly opened the package. She was curious to see the pictures that she had forgotten to pick up. It was nice that the place she had been using ever since she was a little girl was nice enough to forward her work to her. She ripped the envelope open and there to her surprise was a grotesque picture enclosed. She stared at it horrified. Paralyzed with fear, unable to speak or move. The picture fell to the floor. *Who could have sent this? Lock the doors.* She ran to the front door and checked the locks and then to the back and verandas. There was a noise outside. *Was she being spied on?* She crept up to the kitchen window and slowly raised her head hoping not to be seen. She surveyed the grounds as far as she could see. There was no one in sight. *Maybe it was an animal knocking over something. She needed to talk to someone.* Megan was shaking as she picked up the phone to call Lulu.

"Hi honey, didn't we talk a few minutes ago? What's up?"

Megan was crying.

"Megan honey, what's going on?"

"Lulu I just received a **package** and it's horrible!"

"Megan honey, calm down and tell Lulu what was in it. Take your time."

"It's a picture of a rag doll hanging from a rope and at the bottom written in blood is scrawled *MEGAN*. Someone is trying to frighten me and they're doing a good job."

"Megan honey, stay calm. Take my advice and don't tell anyone about this until we can figure it out. Promise?"

"Yes, I promise, but Lulu I am scared."

"Don't worry we'll get to the bottom of this. I'm coming right over."

"Hurry!"

"I will."

Megan sat quietly on the sofa in the great room. She didn't even want to turn on the television. The house was eerily quiet and her heart raced as she waited for what seemed like an eternity. She jumped as the doorbell rang. It was Lulu. "Megan open up, it's me, Lulu." She ran to the door and unlocked it. She ran into his arms and clung to him.

"Honey, you're cold and shaking." He held her tight. She composed herself and then she said, "It's over there."

Lulu walked over and he examined the picture. "I'm going to take this with me. I have a friend who is a cop. Do you remember Christopher George? He graduated the year before we did. I'll show it to him and see what he thinks." Lulu had to go and get ready for work and Megan had to finish dinner. After he left, she locked the doors and managed to finish preparing dinner. Shortly after, Jackson and the children came home. Megan was on edge at the dinner table. It was unusual for her not to inquire about the events that occurred in the children's day. Sarah was excited and told every detail without being asked so Megan's look of distress went unnoticed by the children. But Jackson noticed and he asked, "Megan, is everything alright?"

"Yes, I'm fine." She lied. That was the first bold face lie she told Jackson. He didn't believe her but decided not to pry. The days that followed were tense. Megan jumped at the ringing of the doorbell. She approached the door and every delivery with caution. The following weeks were uneventful and Megan forgot about the picture and she began to relax.

As Jackson promised her divorce was quick and a few weeks later the papers came. She set the divorce papers up on her dresser where she could see them as often as she needed to. She couldn't believe that they were real. She went down to the kitchen to begin her day as usual and the phone rang. "Hello!"

"Megan It's me."

"Hi Mama. Is everything alright?"

JANIS BERESFORD-MCLENNAN

"Yes. We haven't seen you for a while."

"I've been busy. The kids homework, music, dance, this job keeps me busy."

"Well you really messed things up. You could have been taking care of your own home instead of slaving in someone else's. Tom is getting married to a nurse at the hospital. After the wedding they're moving to California."

Megan thought, *California, wow! Great! I'll be rid of him for good. I can get rid of this fat suit and live a normal life here with my family and friends.*

Joan continued, "I don't know the nurse he is marrying but I hear that her family is filthy rich. You know that money always marries money. Megan, I have to get something really special to wear to the wedding. "

"Mama, I'm sure that you'll find something exquisite. I wish his new wife well and I hope that she has a better life with him than I did."

Joan was excited to be invited to Tom's wedding, so she ignored Megan's comment. "The wedding will be in two weeks and the elite of this town will be attending."

"What do you want me to say, Mama?"

"What can you say? You had your chance and you blew it. Now someone else will be able to brag about her wonderful husband and about being the wife of a prominent physician."

"If that's the way you see it, I can't change your mind. I have to go. I'll call you later, bye." Megan wondered, *What's wrong with Mama? Why did she accept things from white people that she wouldn't from blacks? What happened in her past to screw her up like this?* Megan loved her parents but she didn't like them and wanted very little to do with them. The mansion by the ocean had become her home and

Jackson and the girls were her family. He consulted her before making any decision concerning his home or his children and he gave her the utmost respect.

———◦《◉》◦———

Life was different for Megan. Nothing had changed physically but it felt as though it did. Everyday was a day of celebration of freedom and she felt joyful. She did what she wanted to do. No one controlled her life and she felt as though she could sprout wings and fly. She and her friends got together often especially Lulu. She wanted to celebrate her new life and good fortune and decided to have her friends over for an evening of fun and laughter. The preparations were done and she was dressed and waiting. A few minutes later the doorbell rang. They had arrived.

"Hi everyone come on in."

They all hugged and kissed. Lizzie was impressed.

"This place is gorgeous. How do you manage to take care of such a huge place all by yourself?"

Jennifer answered Lizzie's question.

"When Jackson placed the responsibility of running this estate in my hands, I hired cleaners to do a thorough cleaning job once a week. All Megan does is the everyday upkeep but she has help."

Lizzie said, "It's still a big responsibility"

"Lizzie it's like working for myself. I basically do what I want and Jackson values my opinion."

"Jackson, values everyone's opinion. That's why we all like working for him."

Lulu sensed that Jennifer wanted to fight with Megan so he disengaged and walked around admiring the décor and the fine art. And then he asked the question that was weighing heavily on his mind. "What would make a woman leave a beautiful home like this?"

Lizzie picked up Jackson's picture and added, "And don't forget this fine ex-husband of hers." Still holding his picture she smacked her lips and said, "This man is fine! By the way, where is he?"

Megan said, "He took his kids and parents to dinner. Lizzie, you would be the one to notice how *fine* he is."

"You bet! He's single and Megan you're single, girl if I were you, I'd be all over him."

Jennifer was irritated with Lizzie. She angrily said, "I know you would. Megan won't do; trust me, I know."

With a smirk, Lizzie turned to Jennifer and said, "Well, Megan may not *do* but I'll do. I'll do anything that fine man tells me to!"

Jennifer ignored Lizzie and turned to Lulu. Michelle left because she couldn't handle the stress of life and she felt guilty. She didn't want any money in the settlement but he supports her anyway. The check goes to her mother, twenty-eight thousand a month. I know, I am the one who makes sure she gets it."

Lulu whistled. "Wow. Lucky bitch!"

"I liked her. She was very nice to me and when she left she asked Jackson to make sure Tom didn't hurt me."

"How did you know that?"

Megan sensed that she and Jennifer were having issues but couldn't figure out exactly what was troubling her friend. Instinctively she lied so Jennifer wouldn't have any idea how close she and Jackson were becoming. "Jackson mentioned that his wife liked me and asked him to help me with the divorce."

"Jackson isn't a divorce lawyer."

"I know, but he looked at the papers to make sure that they were legally correct."

Megan figured that if Jennifer wanted to feel that she was indispensable to Jackson, so be it.

Lulu thought that he would break up this little tiff. "Where's the food? I'm starving."

"I knew that you were coming so I made plenty."

"Ha, ha, ha. You're really funny."

They gathered around the huge island in the kitchen and they began to eat. They ate a lot, talked a lot, and laughed a lot.

Ariel was pensive and Megan was concerned. "Ariel, what's the matter? You're not speaking and we all know that when you play with your food that something is wrong."

"Megan, did you hear that Tom is getting married? The wedding is going to be huge." She bowed her head. "I've been assigned to cover the wedding. Megan I'm sorry, but it's my job."

Before Megan responded, Jennifer had an outburst. "For crying out loud! We helped her to get away from Tom and we got her on her feet. We can't live our lives catering to her. It's your job Ariel, do it!"

"Why are you being such a bitch? Ever since Megan got her divorce you've been an evil bitch! Either come out with it or stop!"

"Lulu this is none of your damn business! Just shut the hell up!"

"No you didn't! I am not Megan! I will kick your ass! You needed to check your nasty ass attitude at the door. If you knew that you were going to be such a bitch, you should've stayed at home."

"Jen, Lulu, guys, I don't want anyone squabbling about me. I am fine with Ariel covering the wedding. Mama called and told me all about it. I really wish the bride well and believe me I will be praying for her."

"My sources at the television station tell me that the Douglas' are a very loving and caring family. Tom will have a hard time if he doesn't change his behavior."

"Maybe that's why he's moving to California."

"He is moving to California? My sources didn't tell me that. Who told you?"

"None other than his best friend and advocate, my loving mother."

Lulu chimed in again. "Your mother and Tom deserve each other. They're the ones who should be married."

They all laughed at the very thought.

"His new wife is in for a big surprise. I'm glad that they're leaving, the sooner the better. Mama and Daddy are going to attend the wedding."

"Why am I not surprised? What's wrong with your mother?"

Lizzie said, "Lulu don't blame Joan. Peter is as much to blame. He doesn't stop her from doing the things she does."

"Lizzie, everyone knows that my father is weak. Let them go. I don't care."

They had a lot of fun that night but Jennifer kept quiet most of the time.

Chapter 21

After dinner Jackson dropped his parents off, and went home. The kids were very tired and they went straight to bed. Jackson wanted a drink and he offered one to Megan, they began talking about their evening and he smiled when he said to Megan, "My mother asked for you."

"Me? I didn't think she liked me."

"She knows that this family cannot live without you."

Megan took offense when Mrs. Montgomery once said to her, "You have a gorgeous face and beautiful hair." Then she deliberately and slowly moved her eyes down Megan's entire body and then as if her thought escaped without permission she said. "At least you dress elegantly. You have a way of putting yourself together nicely."

Jackson smiled as he read Megan's thoughts correctly and said, "Sometimes my mother just opens her mouth. She didn't mean to hurt you."

Megan smiled and then she said. "I am glad that you think that I am doing a good job."

He leaned forward and with a big smile he said. "You know you are."

He trusted her completely. "Megan, you're doing a great job

managing the household accounts, I'm sure that Jennifer is re-lieved not having to manage the finances of my home."

"Jackson, I try to do my best."

"I know."

She got a serious look on her face.

"What's the matter?"

"We're going to have to fire Grant. He and I have been having some serious arguments. He cannot account for a lot of the funds he's been spending. Here." She showed Jackson the accounting books. "I've been keeping tabs on him since I started handling the accounts and he hates it. He's been padding the accounts and he knows that I know. Jackson, he's stealing from you. I'm so sorry."

"Don't be. I suspected that he was stealing but I didn't have the time to look into it. Do you want me to fire him?"

"No. I can handle it."

"Good. I'll make a few calls. I need to fill that position soon."

Later that morning, Megan picked up the phone and dialed Grant's number. "Grant, would you please come up to the house for a moment?"

"Yes, Ma'am." Grant answered, "I'll be right there."

Grant entered the kitchen door and Megan called out to him, "I'm in Jackson's office, come on in."

Grant entered the office and Megan offered him a seat. "Grant, you know why I called you in. Jackson and I have gone over these books and we cannot account for several thousands dollars. Would you care to explain?"

Grant rolled his eyes, "I don't know what you're talking about."

"Grant you and I both know what happened to that money. Unfortunately I'm going to have to let you go."

"*You're* letting me go?"

"Well, yes, I'm letting you go."

"Lady, who the hell do you think you are? YOU can't do anything! I don't work for you!"

Megan's heart began to beat faster. She stammered "I understand that, but Jackson has given me the authority to act in the best interest of this household. You'll be paid for the work you did today. Please make sure you leave the tools in the shed on your way out."

Grant was quiet for a moment. Megan pushed her chair back to leave when suddenly Grant slammed his hand on the desk, "Where the hell do you think you're going? We're not done with this conversation until I say so! I've worked for Mr. Montgomery for years and no fat pig is gonna fire me!"

At that moment, she didn't see Grant standing before her, she saw Tom. Fear gripped her. Her stomach was in knots. *I can't let him intimidate me. I have to stay in control.*

Megan picked the phone up, "As I said, you are fired. Please leave now or I'll call the police."

Kicking his chair aside, Grant said, "This isn't over!" and stormed out.

Megan fell back into her chair and took a deep breath. She was relieved that he was gone.

Chapter 22

"Jackson, there is something I would like to ask you. I want to have my family over. Tom is getting married. He has moved on and I need to straighten out a few things with my family before I can move on too. I need to give them the chance to redeem themselves."

"I understand. I will take the children to dinner and a movie. He was glad that she was moving on with her life. He noticed that she was in very high spirits since the divorce and he was happy for her. He smiled as he thought to himself. *Do I dare declare my feelings for her? How would she react?* As he promised, that night he took the children out so that she could have complete privacy.

It was Friday night and Megan was expecting her grandparents, Aunt Marcia, and her parents for dinner. Megan prepared a lovely dinner and her presentation was nothing but regal. The doorbell rang. She ran to open the door but there was no one there. She looked around but saw no one and as she stepped outside, she stumbled over a box from the florist. Megan excitedly took the box and ran to untie the ribbon and opened the box. She wondered, *who were the flowers from?* She untied the ribbon expecting to see a bouquet of beautiful roses. She dropped the box in horror. *Who would do this?* She had forgotten about the picture and now this, a box of black dead roses and a note that said: These black roses are dead just like you.

Megan shook with fear. She cried. *Who was doing this to her? Who hated her this much?* She didn't think that she had any enemies. With trembling hands she picked up the phone and dialed Lulu's number. "Lulu, it happened again!"

"What happened?"

"I just received a box of dead black roses and a note."

"What? Are you okay?"

"No, I'm not okay! I'm horrified! My family is going to be here any minute and I'm shaking like a leaf."

"Hold on honey, I'll be right over. Make yourself a cup of tea and take a few deep breaths. I'm on my way." Lulu must have broken every traffic rule because he was there in minutes. He knocked at the kitchen door, but Megan refused to open the door. She was like a frightened kitten.

"It's me, Lulu. Megan, open the door."

Megan opened the door and led him to the flowers.

"God! How awful! Who would think of such a hideous thing to do?" He took the box. "Let me see. I'm going to take them with me to Christopher. He is going to get to the bottom of this. His office is downtown, I spoke to him about the picture and I gave it to him. I'll give him a call and see what he thinks about this new development, but honey I don't know what to tell you right now. All I can say is stay calm and try to get through the evening with your family." He held her for a while until she was calm and then the doorbell rang.

Megan jumped.

"I'll get it." Lulu opened the door. Her family had arrived. He kissed her. "I've got to go, I'll call you later."

Megan welcomed her family and for the moment forgot what had happened earlier. Joan had never heard of the Montgomerys and she immediately assumed that they were white. She admired the way they lived. Great financial wealth was evident in this home. Joan walked around admiring the magnificent paintings and sculptures. She loved the floral arrangements; she thought, *this is the life.*

Megan put on a brave face for her family. Her grandmother was very happy to see that old smile. "Honey it's so nice to see you happy. Thank you for inviting us."

"You're welcome, Grandma"

Rose said, "This is the answer to my prayers. I've stayed on my knees and prayed for you everyday since that man put you in the hospital." Rose dared Joan to contradict her with an evil look, but Joan ignored her.

"I made a novena to St. Jude. He is the Saint for impossible cases. Praise Jesus, he did answer because I know that if it were not for answered prayers we would not be here tonight enjoying a wonderful evening with you."

"Grandma, I know that you were praying for me and I thank you."

"Megan, you poor dear, he kept you from the people that love you. Couldn't even make a phone call, but God delivered you and gave you this great job with this wonderful family.

"Grandma, my phone calls were taped and he checked my cell phone. I had to be careful not to make Tom angry. It was easier not to call anyone."

"I know dear. It was the most painful thing not knowing while

I was enjoying myself if you were being abused at that very moment. My poor Megan."

"Rose, stop acting as if Megan was dying. She always had it good. Peter and I provided her with everything she needed. If you ask me, she had a charmed life."

"That's right, Mama I have to thank you for providing me with my husband and a marriage that you thought was wonderful." Megan turned her attention to the others, "That is why I invited all of you here, I want to tell you the details of my marriage. I need to do this. I need to forgive and move on."

"Megan, I don't have time for this. I work hard and when I go out I want to have fun, not be psychoanalyzed." Joan got up to leave, but her husband stood in front of her.

"Joan, sit down, don't move. Our daughter has something to say and you *will* listen!"

Surprise was the expression on the faces of everyone but Joan was the one most surprised. She sat down.

Megan spoke in a very controlled tone. "Grandma and Grandpa I don't want to be disrespectful but what I am about to tell you is not only vulgar but sinful."

"I can take it honey. If you can survive it, I can hear it."

"Thanks Grandma."

Megan told them in detail about the marriage but she never mentioned the tapes. She didn't trust her mother. Her grandparents listened with stoned faces as they heard her first sexual experience and the next morning, and the next day, and so on, and so on.

Marcia was crying. "My poor baby! Megan honey, why didn't you do this when you came back from your honeymoon?"

"I did! I went to my wonderful parents who always provided

what I needed and I showed them the bruises and I begged them to help me! Daddy walked out and my loving mother told me to handle my business quietly and not put her job in jeopardy. She said that part of being a woman is handling your own business and she continued to be friends with Tom. I never understood what kind of hold he had on you, Mama."

"I hate when you call me that."

"God Joan! What kind of mother are you? No! What kind of human being are you? Peter what happened to you? We were so close as children. You were a strong man. You didn't worry about life but you got serious when it mattered."

"Marcia, I don't have any excuses. I just stopped fighting. I am so sorry darling, your whole life I have let you down but this; this was unforgivable of me. I wouldn't be surprised if you never talked to me again."

"Daddy, I forgive you. I love you but I have to be honest I don't trust you. I needed you to protect me. I needed you to stop Tom." She tried to hold back the tears.

"Daddy, you sat down and ate and drank with him. And even after the divorce you went to his wedding. How could you? How could you celebrate with the man you knew was hurting me? How could you, Daddy?" She was shaking and crying uncontrollably.

Rose's face was drenched with tears and Marcia wept bitterly.

Marcia yelled, "Oh my God! Oh my God! She was married to the prince of darkness himself, and Joan, you helped him!"

Peter Sr.'s face was like stone and he sat motionless as if he were watching a movie. Grimacing he said, "I could kill that man."

And Rose said, " I feel the same way."

"Tom is a physician. He came from old money. From what he tells me his parents traveled all over the world while he was growing up. Maybe their lack of interest affected him in a negative way. Peter, if you had talked to Tom like a man maybe he would have listened. But you didn't have the guts."

"Joan! Are you blaming me? You don't consult me about anything! You do exactly what you want and when things turn out wrong I have to endure your constant badgering. Maybe there was more that I could have done. I am sorry that this turned out the way it did, Megan, I am, but you can't blame me for this Joan! You can't still be making excuses for him! You just can't! When I think how much I love you. I want to commit myself into an insane asylum and I ask myself the questions daily. How could I have fallen in love with you and why can't I stop loving you? The only good thing that came from our marriage is Megan." Peter with tears in his eyes said. "Megan, I am sorry. I am so sorry. I promise that I'll make it up to you if it takes the rest of my life."

Joan got up. "I am not going to stay here and take this abuse."

"Joan, you had better get a grip! The only family you have is Peter and Megan. It's never too late. You need to start being a mother to this child."

"Shut up Marcia. Maybe if you had a family of your own, you would stay out of mine."

Rose had enough. She got up and walked over to her daughter-in-law.

"What is it with you? At first I thought that you were a new mother and didn't know how to take care of this child, so I helped. Then I realized that you had no connection to this beautiful child. There are women in this world who can't have a child and you hate yours. I've tried to hate you. After my son married you, I watched him change from a decent human being to a sad excuse of a man. For some reason, God has put a profound love in me for you. God help me Joan, I love you. Do you hear me? I love you but I don't understand how you could be so cold and hateful."

"Cold and hateful! You think that I'm cold and hateful? What do you know about me? You sit on your high horse judging me." The tears flowed like a faucet from Joan's eyes, her lips trembled and she began to speak, "I hated my mother. She was a whore! She was the meanest black human being I ever encountered. She hated me, her only girl child. I don't know who my father is. The men she dated were men who partied, did drugs, alcohol, cheated with other women and had no problems trying to have sex with me. I had to constantly be aware of them and what they were thinking about me." She gritted her teeth. Anger heaved in her chest, and the words spewed out. "I hate anything or anyone that looks black! I left home. I left her and my four younger brothers. I kept running and I never looked back."

Joan wiped away the tears that flooded her eyes and with a clear view she saw Peter and his family standing around her with looks of great compassion on their faces. She knew that their hearts genuinely ached for her. She felt their love and acceptance.

Encouraged by this, she stood up and reached for her husband and spoke directly to him. "Peter, I am so sorry. I made your life a living hell. I really do love you and I want to thank you for putting up with me all these years."

"I love you too, Joan. I don't know why, but no matter how hard I tried I couldn't stop loving you."

Although Joan was moved, she still did not understand her

daughter's distress and her need to leave Tom. In her opinion he was still a good catch. He was a physician and he came from a wealthy family. What more could anyone want?

The events of the evening made Rose tired and she was ready to leave. She kissed her granddaughter; and with a sweet smile, she said, "Goodnight, my darling." Rose grabbed her husband's hand and said, "Let's go, honey." There was a determination in her facial expression that they all recognized. Some healing was accomplished tonight, and they knew that if Rose had anything to do with it, there was more to come.

Chapter 23

The next day Megan was up early and dressed. Megan brewed a fresh pot of coffee and sat on the veranda with a steaming hot cup. It was a quiet and peaceful Saturday morning. The sun rose over the gushing waves of the ocean that lashed against the rocks. It was so inviting. She could understand why Jackson swam every morning before breakfast but he was nowhere to be seen. Maybe he wanted to sleep in. As she viewed the scenery, she reflected on her life and was grateful for her father's family and her friends. Her grandmother was more like a mother to her. As for Aunt Marcia, Megan couldn't even begin to describe her love for her. There were times she wished that Marcia was her birth mother. *Oh my! It's getting late I should get started before the children get up.* She prepared a big breakfast for the family.

"Good morning, something smells good."

She turned to see her boss standing in the doorway of the kitchen.

"Hi Jackson, I'll go up and get the children so that we can sit and eat together."

"They're not here. Last night after the movie I took them over to my parents. I thought that you might need some time to yourself after meeting with your family." He sat down at the kitchen island. "How did that go?"

She poured him a cup of coffee. "Do you want to eat in here or do you want to eat at the dining table?"

"Here is good."

She proceeded to fix him a plate. "It went well. My father and mother surprised me, but the rest of it went exactly as I expected. The important thing is that I got it all out."

"Good. There is something that I want to ask you."

She turned to face him and a gentle smile was on his face.

"I want to ask you to marry me."

Shock registered on her face. She was confused and didn't know what to say, "What? Big, fat, old me?" She laughed a nervous laugh. All the degrading things Tom told her came rushing back now. *Who would want me? He doesn't even know what I really look like. He is probably feeling sorry for me. Why would he want to marry me? I'm just a glorified maid.*

His deep and powerful voice brought her mind back to the subject at hand. "It's not a joke. I am serious. Listen and hear me out. You are a wonderful woman and I'm in love with you. My heart skips a beat when I see you coming in my direction. I love you just the way you are. If you want to lose the weight, you can lose it for yourself but you don't need to lose it for me. I know from what you told me about your marriage to Tom that it might be difficult for you to trust anyone. We don't have to have a sexual relationship now. I will wait until you are ready, no rush, I promise." Jackson kept his eyes firmly on her, and made her look him directly in the face.

Jackson was a good father to his children and a wonderful friend to her. Megan had developed deep feelings for him but she had sworn off men, since Tom. The wounds of that relationship were deep. She had to admit that she often admired Jackson's tall and lean body when he came up from his swim and while he stood on the terrace drinking his morning coffee. She loved the way he focused on the gushing waves of the ocean when he was trying to solve a problem. He was truly handsome and that made her wonder why he would want her. His ex-wife was a real beautiful woman and Jen said that he preferred white women. She fidgeted, she had fallen in love with him but didn't dare admit it. Look at what happened when she declared her love for Tom. "Jackson you don't know me. I am not who you think I am."

"What do you mean?'

"I have deceived you. I have lied to you. And when I tell you the truth you might ask me to leave but I can't continue to lie to you. You have been too good to me. As I told you, Tom was physically and sexually abusive to me. What I didn't tell you was that I realize that he hated fat people so I gained fifty pounds. Lulu designed a fat body suit for me and I lost the weight I gained but I continued wearing the fat body suit. I plan to stop wearing it after Tom moves to California. I'm so sorry that I lied to you but I believed that my life depended on it. I can understand if you are angry and want me to leave."

He stayed quiet throughout everything she had to say and then he said, "Megan, if you want to find an excuse not to marry me, say so, but don't presume that I won't forgive you for doing something that saved your life and had nothing to do with me. You did what you needed to do to survive."

"And you are okay with that?"

"I'm not Tom."

"I know Jackson. I know that you're not Tom. If you still want me I'll marry you but I need to continue to wear this body suit until Tom leaves."

"I understand, and yes, I'll have you."

A voice called out, Jackson, we're here." His parents brought the children home. Jackson opened the kitchen door and Megan got coffee mugs. "Hello Mr. and Mrs. Montgomery, May I offer you a cup of coffee?"

Mrs. Montgomery said, "No thank you dear, we just had breakfast. We are not staying we just wanted to drop the children off on our way to the club."

Jackson said, "Dad, I need to talk to you about the Bryson Account."

"Son, you know that I don't talk business when I'm with my family."

"Yes Sir, but I need to see you first thing Monday morning. I have to close this deal."

"Monday morning it is. Come on, my love, let's go." He smiled and said, "I have a hot date with my wife."

After his parents left, Jackson told the children the good news. They were happy. Their love for Megan made it easy for them to accept her.

Christine said, "May I be in the wedding?" Sarah said, " Me too!" and Jacob said "Me too!"

"You are all going to be in the wedding but it's our little secret. Jackson, I want a very small ceremony in the garden with our family and our very close friends."

"Whatever you want, my love."

Megan ran to the phone and called her friends. She told them that she needed to see them right away. Their minds went straight to Tom. What happened? They wondered. Lulu was the first to arrive and the others were right behind him. "What's the urgency? What's going on?"

"Come in. Come on in."

Jackson stood close to Megan. Putting his arms around her waist, he drew her tight to him. Surprised looks were on every face. He looked very happy and in a carefree way he said. "I'm taking orders for drinks"

"Martinis all around." Replied a puzzled Lulu.

Jackson got the drinks and then he said. "I think that you are the ones I have to ask for Megan's hand in marriage." He waited. All the while Megan was giggling like a teenager.

Jennifer looked red in the face. She did all she could to keep from screaming and attacking Megan but instead she smiled and said, "You never told us that you were having an affair with the boss?"

"No. Jen, I wasn't."

Jackson was excited and he said anxiously, "Well, is someone going to answer me?"

Her friends were happy, that is everyone, except Jennifer. But Megan was so happy she hadn't noticed. Lulu and Lizzie liked Jackson and thought that he would be the one to restore Megan's faith in men. "Yes. Yes."

Jennifer was silent. The blood had rushed to her face but only Lulu seemed to notice.

Jackson fell to his knees and pulled out the biggest diamond Megan had ever seen. He bought the ring and had been holding onto it for the past two months.

"Megan, I love you. Will you marry me?"

She laughed. "Yes!"

Jackson would have liked to hear her say the words "I love you", but he was patient. He placed the ring on her finger and it was a perfect fit. His lips claimed hers for the first time in a passionate kiss. Her surrender surprised him. He didn't want to stop, but he did. He thought that her response may have been because her friends were there.

Jennifer bowed her head.

"Jen, are you okay?"

"Yes, Lulu."

Jackson said, "Good, because I am taking all of you to dinner to celebrate our engagement."

Jennifer rubbed her forehead as if she was trying to rub her headache away. "I'll have to take a rain-check, I have a migraine. I need to go home and lay in the dark."

Oh Jen, I'm so sorry you're not feeling well. I really wanted you here to celebrate with us. You were right about Tom but you know Jackson so well and I know that this time you will be happy for me. Will you be my maid of honor?"

"I really have to go." Without another word Jennifer ran out of the mansion to her car and left. The others went to dinner but Megan was very concerned about Jennifer. "I hope that Jen is alright."

Lulu said to Megan, "Don't worry she will be."

Chapter 24

They all enjoyed their meal and had a few drinks and Megan enlisted the help of her two friends but they were sworn to secrecy. Lizzie assured Megan that she would have the bridal gown and the children dresses done in time for the wedding. They had a very nice evening together.

Sunday morning Jackson and Megan took the children to church and thanked God for their blessings.

After Jackson left for work Monday morning Lulu and his friend Christopher George arrived.

"Megan, you remember Chris?"

"Yes. Hi how are you?"

"I'm fine. Lulu told me what was going on, and he brought the picture and the box of flowers. We couldn't find any fingerprints. Whoever is doing this is being very careful. Tell me, beside your ex-husband, do you know anyone who would want to harm you?" "No. Not that I could think of. Except ... " Megan started to say something and then she shook her head and said, "No."

"What? Megan, please tell me, everyone and everything is important."

"Well, there was the grounds man and his staff. He was in his thirties. He managed the maintenance of the mansion and the care of the grounds. After I began to keep the books I found out that he was stealing big time from Jackson. When I confronted him he became disrespectful and I fired him. He was very angry. He called me vicious names, and cussed, and threatened me but I didn't take him seriously."

"We have to take everyone seriously. What was his name?"

Everyone calls him by his last name, Grant. His name is Jason Grant."

"I'll have to investigate this but is there anyone else?"

"Yes, but she, it was nothing. Um, well there was a part-time caregiver that I also fired. She took care of Mrs. Montgomery when I did errands."

"What happened?"

"She was insolent. She refused to take orders from me, so I fired her."

"How did she take it?"

"She was obviously upset but she left quietly."

"I need their full names and addresses and any other information you have."

"I'll get that for you. Thank you guys for your help. Where are my manners? May I offer anyone some coffee or a sandwich?"

"No honey, I have to be going."

"How about you, Chris?"

"No thank you."

Megan returned with the information Chris asked for.

"Here is my card. Megan, if you think of anything, anything at all, no matter how unimportant you think it is, call me. In the mean time I'll step up the patrol cars in this area. It was nice seeing you again, Megan. I'll be in touch soon. I promise that we'll get to the bottom of this."

Lulu held Megan's hand. "Honey, I think that it is very important that you do not forget to wear this fat suit. I know that you are busy with the wedding plans but don't take any chances."

"I know. I won't forget. I didn't plan to."

Jennifer did not go into work that morning but sent her resignation by messenger. Jackson didn't know what to make of it so he called Megan. "Hi, honey."

"Hello Jackson, miss me already?"

"Yes I do, but that is not why I am calling."

"What happened? You sound upset."

"I'm more puzzled than upset. Jennifer quit today. She didn't come in to work. Her letter came by messenger."

Megan was quiet.

"Megan, honey, did you know about this?

"No! Jackson, but Lulu believes that Jen is in love with you."

"Nonsense, I have never given Jennifer any reason to believe that I had any romantic interest in her."

"I know, honey. I'm afraid that I may have lost a friend and you an excellent assistant." Megan knew Jennifer. She knew that their friendship was definitely going to change. She would give Jen some time and then she would have a talk with her after the wedding and things had settled down. She had other things on her mind. She could no longer keep what was happening from Jackson. He trusted her and she had to tell him about the picture, the flowers and about what Detective Christopher George was doing.

"Jackson I don't mean to change the subject but I need to speak with you on a very serious matter."

"Something wrong?"

"Yes, but it will wait until you get home. It's not something that can be discussed over the telephone. I have a few errands to run. See you at dinner. "

"I love you. Bye." He was still waiting for those words but they didn't come. Jackson felt an icy chill when he hung up the phone. He shivered and returned to the work on his desk.

Chapter 25

The wedding was going to be in three weeks and again her best friend was not going to be a part of it. Detective Christopher George warned her to keep her plans under wraps. She had to have the invitations hand delivered to both families and to their closest friends. Everyone was invited to a formal garden party with no mention of the wedding. She had better get busy. She gathered her purse and everything she needed as she checked off the things on her mental list. *Jackson pulled some strings and got the license, the church, and the minister to perform the ceremony and he will take care of his and little Jacob's Tuxedos. Jacob is going to be the ring bearer and the girls are going to be the bride's maids. All the plans are made and everything should be in place soon.* With everything in hand, Megan ran to her car and drove out of the driveway.

She had driven three blocks when she realized that the car was going too fast down the hill leading to the main road. Megan braked, but the car kept speeding down the hill. Her heart was beating fast. Panic and fear rose up in her chest. The car careened around the bend and sped down the road. The color drained from her face. "Oh God! Oh God! I don't want to die! Lord help me! Please help me!" She tried shifting gears but the engine did not respond, she pumped the brakes but the car went faster. She was headed into traffic on the main street. Tears streamed down her cheeks. The glare from the sun blinded her and she began to lose control of the car. The car swayed from one side of the street to the other.

"Oh God what am I going to do?" On both sides of the street were mansions but no one in sight. These homes were far apart. Hopefully, she could think of something by the time she reached the end of that road. She turned the staring wheel hand over hand. Her foot was off the gas pedal but the car continued down the long winding road at a very fast speed. There it was, a thick hedge that rimmed the hidden estate up ahead. Her only chance was to run the car into it. She closed her eyes in anticipation of the crash. The car flew into the hedge. It spun around and then stopped. There was no physical damage done to the car or to her.

Her entire body was shaking. Megan leaned her head on the staring wheel and thanked God that she was still alive. After she calmed herself a little, she took out her cell and with panted breath she called Lulu.

"Megan? I can't understand what you are saying!"

"Oh God Lulu! He wants to kill me!"

"Megan, calm down! What happened?"

"The car! The brakes failed! I almost got killed!"

"Oh my God. Honey, I'm on my way!"

Lulu kept talking to her while he got into the car and while he was driving to where she was. Megan, you have to tell Jackson. It's getting very serious."

"I know. I planned to tell him tonight. That was before this. I'll call him now." She got off the phone and called Jackson and in a very shaken voice she told him everything.

"Megan, why didn't you tell me this before?"

"I don't know. I thought that it would just stop."

"I'm on my way home and I want to talk to that Detective. I have all the information he needs on Grant."

Lulu got there first. He called the tow truck and he took Megan home. Jackson arrived shortly after they did. He ran to her, "Honey, are you alright?"

He hugged her and she held him tight. He wanted to comfort her, he felt that it was his job to protect her.

Lulu made coffee and some sandwiches but Megan couldn't eat. Detective Christopher George arrived and after meeting Jackson, he took Megan's statement and promised Jackson that he was doing all he could. The police cars patrolled the area and they saw nothing unusual.

Jackson looked him in his eyes. "My family is in danger and I want something done to find out who is behind this!"

"Look, I would feel the same way if it were my family, but let me check out this hunch I have. I'm hoping to come up with some answers soon. We are checking out everyone who could possibly be a suspect."

⚬

In the days that followed things quieted down. No more incidents. Megan was going to try to relax she had a few appointments and some last minute plans. The wedding was a week away. Jackson went everywhere with her and never let her out of his sight.

The staff working on the grounds had not arrived as yet. Jackson left for the office, he had an appointment with an important client. He wanted to cancel but Megan begged him not to. He warned her.

"Don't leave the mansion. Promise me. I will be back as soon and I can."

Megan agreed not to go out but she refused to let anyone take her power away from her. She was not going to be afraid anymore. Jackson left for the office. She was in the kitchen cleaning up the breakfast dishes. She felt a presence and thought that Jackson had forgotten something but she turned around only to see Tom standing with a butcher knife in his hands. His ice-cold blue eyes glared at her. He looked like a possessed man and there was an eerie quietness about him. Megan was scared. She was keenly aware that domestic violence often ended in death. "Tom! What are you doing here?

He didn't answer, under that fat suit was a beautiful shapely body. She fooled him into thinking that she was a 200-pound whale. All the while, she was the magnificent creature he married. She belonged to him.

Jackson is upstairs."

"Lying bitch! I have been watching this place and saw when he left for the office. You have created a nice little love nest here. You're a whore! You lying bitch! Your friend Jennifer told me of your schemes to leave me. She said that she and the others helped you. I was such a damn fool, falling for that fat suit. I got to give it to you. You really had me going, I even felt pity for you."

The phone rang. It was Lulu calling. When Jackson was not with Megan, Lulu was a stand in. The night before Jackson told Lulu that he had the appointment but was considering not going. It was unusual for Megan not to answer the phone at this time of the morning. Megan ignored the ringing and tried to talk Tom down.

"Tom, you are married now and have a different life. Why are you bothering with me? You don't need to do this."

"Honey when I'm finished with you they're not going to recognize you."

"Tom stop! Think about your career and your new wife. Leave now and I won't tell anyone. I promise."

"You promise? Don't worry, I know that you won't tell anyone anything. I am going to kill you."

Lulu was calling her cell phone now which distracted Tom for a second.

She started screaming and ran to the front door. He ran behind her. She struggled but the door was locked and she couldn't get it opened and he was gaining on her. She looked up the stairway leading to the bedrooms, but she would really be trapped there. She doubled back into the family room and back into the kitchen. He was right behind her. She fell and he grabbed her and he dragged her across the floor, "Bitch, I am going to enjoy killing you."

She lay on her back and he was on top of her. It was difficult holding her down, the suit kept slipping out of his hand. He held both of her hands with his, he let go of one hand and he stabbed her. He pulled out the knife to repeat the action but she knocked the knife out of his hand. She scratched his face while he tried to retrieve the knife. Megan fought for her life. She broke free from his grip and tried to open the back door, but he grabbed her. She screamed, and he slapped her hard. He plunged the knife into her again and he pinned her down again. As he was about to bring the knife down a third time Jackson knocked him across his head with a bottle of white wine that was on the counter top. He didn't want to take his eyes off Tom. "Are you hurt?"

"No, thank God for this suit, the knife got stuck in it. It was too thick."

Jackson picked up the phone.

"Jackson, no, don't call the cops. Just let him go."

"Are you crazy?"

"He'll be leaving for California soon, just let him go."

"I don't like this. At least let me call Christopher." He speed dialed Christopher.

"Hi, Jackson!"

"Tom's here, he tried to kill Megan and she still doesn't want to press charges."

"Jackson, I'll be right over."

Jackson made another call to his attorney and best friend. Just then Lulu arrived.

"What's going on here?"

"He tried to kill Megan"

"Jackson, excuse me but there is something I need to do. I'll be right back."

Lulu got an old tin can Jacob played with on the back lawn. He handed it to Megan. "Go on, pee in it. I hope your bladder is full." Megan hesitated but a stern look from Lulu convinced her. She went into the bathroom and she peed. Lulu took the can from her. He and Jackson dragged Tom outside to the gate. Lulu slowly poured Megan's urine in Tom's face. Drenched in Megan's urine, Tom immediately became conscious.

"You evil pig, this is what pigs get and this is for my best friend."

Jackson took over and angrily threatened Tom. "Let me make this very clear, leave Megan alone! If you don't, I am going to make sure that your license is revoked and I will make your life a living hell. I have already started the process and if anything happens to anyone in my family you are going down." His attorney was still on the phone "Henry are you still there?"

"Yes Jackson, I'm here."

"Henry, I have you on speaker, and I want you to tell Tom Brinkley what will happen to him if he doesn't leave Meagan alone."

Henry Bingham was a reputable attorney so Tom knew of him. Henry did as Jackson requested. Tom really was a coward. He was face to face with a rich and powerful man who could easily ruin his entire life. He was very angry that Megan had outsmarted him and there was nothing that he could do to her.

Jackson shouted, "Get the hell off my property now and don't you ever let me see your hateful face around here again!" Jackson kicked him out and locked the iron gates to his mansion. Tom left before the detective arrived.

Christopher arrived and he asked Jackson, "Why did you let him go?"

Jackson replied, "I told you that we are not going to press charges."

"Jackson, it doesn't matter if you want to press charges or not we have to arrest him. He committed a crime."

"Christopher go ahead but keep Megan out of it, if you can."

Christopher went to Tom's apartment and arrested him. Tom made bail and was let go. He was angry and consumed with a destructive desire and someone had to pay.

Chapter 26

Jackson got on the phone and within one hour the mansion was surrounded with several guards and a schedule was made for round the clock guards.

"Lulu, would you please do me a favor and stay here with Megan? I have to run an errand. I'll be back soon."

Jackson got into his car and dialed Jennifer's number.

"Hello Jackson."

"Jennifer, I need to speak with you."

"Jackson, I'm not coming back."

"Jennifer, I really need to see you."

"Alright Jackson, I'm at home, my address is 222 Melanie Lane, just off Ventura."

"I know where that is. I'm on my way."

Jennifer ran upstairs and took a quick shower and got dressed. She fixed her hair and makeup. She went downstairs, and put on a pot of coffee, and took out the croissants and butter. She was ready to entertain her ex-boss when she heard the doorbell.

"Just a minute, I'm coming!"

She opened the door and a broad smiled appeared on her face. She thought that he had come to convince her that he needed her and wanted her to return to work immediately.

"Hello, Jackson. Come in"

Jackson entered the house and stood by the door. The look on his face was disdain.

"They say that hell hath no fury like a woman's scorn. Well, you have proven that. I always thought of you as a good person but you are as evil as they come."

"Jackson, what are you talking about?"

"Tom almost killed your best friend this morning! Lulu called me as I was driving to a meeting with a client. He said that you were having frequent conversations with Lizzie. He also said that your questions were mainly about Megan, me, and our wedding. He saw you and Tom at a restaurant in deep conversation. You didn't see him, so he stood outside and watched. He said that you and Tom spoke for over an hour. He didn't want to frighten Megan so he called me. I was at the gas station a few blocks away from home and after talking to Lulu, I remembered that I saw a car parked across the street from the mansion. I didn't see anyone in it, and just out of habit, I wrote down the tag number. I called a friend of mine at DMV and guess whose car it was? I got home just in time to stop him from killing Megan."

"Jackson, I swear I didn't think that he would hurt her!"

"What the hell did you think he would do? You disgust me. I never want to ever see you again."

Jackson turned to leave but Jennifer grabbed his arm.

"Let go!" He pulled away.

"Jackson, please don't say that. I love you. I am your equal not her. I know everything about you. I know what you need and what you like. I have served you with all my heart. Jackson, I saw how burdened you were with Michelle. Who do you think prodded her to leave? She and I talked everyday and she kept saying that she couldn't cope. I told her what she was doing to you and the kids was wrong. I reasoned with her and showed her that the best thing she could do for you and the children was to leave. I was the one who took her home to her parents."

"You did what? I can't believe what I am hearing. Do you hear yourself? How dare you? You had no right!"

"I had every right. She wanted to go anyway, she just needed a little help in making up her mind. You need a wife that could make you happy."

"And I guess that would be you."

"Yes, I would have made you happy. Megan doesn't deserve you." She laughed a wicked laugh. "This is classic, the boss marrying his maid. Jackson we worked together and we would make a great team at work and home."

She pleaded and her eyes were so sincere.

"You are insane!"

Jackson walked out and slammed the door behind him, he didn't want to hear anymore. He felt sick. Jennifer ran after him.

"Jackson, don't go. I love you."

He kept on walking out of her life.

The next morning Jackson went into the office to do some work and clean up his desk. Megan and the girls were at the spa. She was safe with the bodyguard he assigned to her. He planned to work from his home office until Tom left for California and he needed some files. His new assistant buzzed him.

"Mr. Montgomery the police are here. They say that they need to speak to you."

"Send them in."

Two detectives entered his office.

"May I help you?"

"Are you Jackson Montgomery?"

Jackson didn't know what to think. "Yes."

The detective flashed her badge. "We have a warrant for your arrest for the assault of Jennifer Bradley, your ex- employee."

"What? I never touched her."

"Sir, I'm going to have to ask you to come down to the station with us."

Jackson's father came into his office. "Jackson what's going on?"

"Dad I don't know, they say that Jennifer has accused me of assault."

"What? I'll call Henry. Jackson's father and his attorney arrived at the stationhouse together. They talked to the police captain and Jackson gave his statement and he was released and the investigators began their investigation.

Jackson returned to the office and called Lulu he did not want to upset Megan.

"Hello Jackson."

"Lulu I have a problem."

"What happened?"

"Apparently Jennifer is in the hospital, she is badly hurt and she claims that I did it."

"That bitch! I told you that she would try to destroy your relationship."

"Lulu, she was my assistant for five years and I never knew her to be vindictive. She is Megan's best friend. I don't know what to do. I don't want Megan to hear about this. I'm not going to tell her until I have to. Lulu, I swear I didn't touch that woman."

"Jackson I believe you. I will get as much information as I can and I'll be careful not to tell Megan. I'll call you back."

Lulu called Lizzie. "Hi Lizzie." But before he could say anything Lizzie burst out talking.

"Lulu? It's Jen, Jackson almost killed her. She is badly hurt."

"Lizzie you're not taking that bitch's side, are you?"

"Then how do you explain it?"

"I don't know but I don't believe that Jackson could hurt a fly. He is not like that. Lizzie, you and I have been friends for a while. You are loyal to a fault. Its okay if you are on Jen's side, but you have to give Megan the same consideration as you will to Jen. Megan doesn't know about this and her wedding is in a week. Please don't spoil this for her, she's had enough problems. Let her have a happy day."

"I can't! I can't let Megan make the same mistake twice. That bastard should go to jail for what he did to Jen."

"Did Jen tell you that she told Tom about our plans to help Megan get her divorce? Did she tell you that Tom almost killed Megan yesterday?"

"No! You lie!"

"I swear to God. I am not lying. That's why Jackson went to see her and I believe him when he said that he did not touch her. Jen is evil, but if you want to find out for yourself so be it. Remember mum's the word."

"I promise I'll wait."

"Good."

Jackson sat at his desk. It was just as he left it the day before. Nothing had been done. *What was he going to do?* This could be big trouble for him. He had seen a glimpse of the evil Jennifer but this was more than he could have imagined. A knock came at his office door. Without looking he said, "Come in."

"Good afternoon Mr. Montgomery."

Surprised he looked up. "Good afternoon Detective."

Mr. Montgomery Sr., saw the detectives and he followed them into his son's office.

"Jackson, is everything alright?"

"Dad, I'm about to find out."

"Sir, all the charges have been dropped."

Jackson cupped his face and breathe a sigh of relief and then he listened.

"A neighbor across the street confirmed the time you said that you visited the victim. She saw you arrive and leave ten minutes later just as you stated. Also your new assistant said that you were on the phone with him on your way there; and he held on for you until you returned to your car ten minutes later. He said that you were giving him instructions for some account that needed to be prepped and assigned to another attorney. You got to the residence at 2:30 and left at 2:45. Jennifer called the police at 3:30 and the doctors said that she would have bled to death had she been injured in that time span. Apparently she waited five minutes before the ambulance arrived, opened the door and bashed her head into the glass door of the grandfather clock in her living room. If she was pushed the way she claims she was, she would have fallen backward but instead she was face down and there were many other indicators that proved that she was lying."

"Thank you, officer."

"I am sorry to put you through what we did but we were just doing our job."

"I understand." He walked the detectives out.

His father hugged him. "I'm not going to ask you why you were visiting that woman but I hope that you have learned your lesson. Son, we have to be very careful especially with ex-employees. Thank God that things turned out well this time."

———◦◦◦———

Lulu and Lizzie were visiting Jennifer but they did not let on that they knew what she did with Tom. The detectives arrived at Jennifer's hospital room.

"May we speak with you alone?"

"Detective you can speak. These are my friends."

"Are you sure?"

"Yes, I'm sure."

"Alright. We have dropped the charges you brought against Mr. Montgomery."

"What? You can't do that. He almost killed me."

"No Ma'am. You almost killed yourself and charges will be brought against you for filing a false report. We recommend that you be evaluated by a psychiatrist."

Lizzie slumped back down in her chair, shocked and unable to believe her ears. Jen was her friend and she realized that she didn't know her at all but Lulu had the satisfaction of saying

"I told you so."

Lizzie spoke through trembling lips. "Jen, how could you? We trusted you! I thought you loved Megan?" Tears flowed down Lizzie's flushed cheeks and she picked up her bag and walked out.

Lulu stayed behind to confront Jennifer. "You were the one that sent the picture and flowers to Megan? You almost killed her in that car."

Jennifer turned and looked Lulu in his face. "It didn't work, did it? I tried to scare her, but nothing I did worked. I thought she would think that it was Tom and run away. She was planning to leave after her divorce, but she didn't. Megan had no right. Jackson belongs to me, not her. That's why I went to Tom."

Lulu got up and locked the door. He jumped on top of Jennifer and he slapped her so hard his hand hurt. "You bitch, you hateful bitch! I wished that you had killed yourself and saved us the trouble of having to look at your sorry ass!"

Lizzie was waiting outside for Lulu. "What took you so long, Lulu?"

"I had something to settle with her." Lulu was rubbing his hand like it hurt.

"Lulu, are you alright?"

"I am now."

Chapter 27

The day of the wedding arrived. It was a beautiful sunny day. The flower gardens, trees and shrubs were satiated with vibrant color. The atmosphere was festive and everyone was too busy to remember the past weeks of unfortunate events. Jackson was finally going to have a normal life with the woman he loved. The children ran around happy, anxiously awaiting the afternoon's festivities.

Jackson for a brief moment reflected on Michelle, his high school sweetheart. Jackson grew up in an environment where the only black person in his life was his father. The exclusive private schools he attended were no exception. He and Michelle grew up in that environment and their parents were very good friends. He hoped that Michelle would find the happiness he had with Megan. Jennifer may have helped her to make her mind up but he knew that she wanted to go for a very long time and truthfully he needed her to go. The marriage was over and she had become another child in his care.

He was happy and his heart leaped with joy at the sight of Megan and at the sound of her voice. The children loved their new mom. Most of the memories they had of Michelle was of violence or depression. Rarely was she normal and when she was, everyone waited for the other shoe to drop.

———=»《O》«=———

Security was positioned around the grounds and warned to keep out of sight. Everyone arrived on time and was seated in the Roman garden. The life sized sculptered statues stood on tall pedestals and surrounded this beautiful garden that was professionally decorated for the wedding. The staff Jackson hired did a fantastic job in the very short time they had to work with.

"What's going on? Mom, did Megan tell you anything?"

"Marcia, your father and I are in the dark like you are."

"Mom, you and Megan talk everyday. Did she tell you what this party was about?"

"No Marcia! She didn't!"

Marcia knew when to leave her mother alone. Just then the usher walked up to them.

"Peter? You are Peter, Sr. and Rose is your wife?"

"Yes."

"Your grand-daughter sent me to get the two of you."

Peter, Sr. and Rose got up to follow her and Joan got up and began to walk behind them.

"Ma'am, I have strict orders, the only people I'm to accompany upstairs to see the bride are Rose and Peter Sr. Please go back to your seat."

"Bride? What bride? Peter, do you know what he is talking about?"

Peter shook his head. "No."

"Ma'am, please sit down."

Her grandparents went up to Megan's room. The guests talked among themselves. Rose and her husband's eyes were wide with surprise and their mouths were wide opened. It was Megan and she was slim and beautiful in a beautiful bridal gown.

"Honey, what's going on?"

"Grandma, Papa, Jackson and I are getting married. He is a good man. Papa I want to ask you to walk me down the aisle."

"I understand honey and I'm proud to do it."

"Why all the secrecy, and where did all that weight go?"

"Grandma, it's a long story. We didn't want Tom to get wind of our plans so we kept it from everyone. He found out anyway and a few days ago he tied to kill me."

"What! Oh my God!"

"Jackson saved my life and warned him to stay away. I really don't want to talk about Tom. I will explain about him and the weight loss later. Megan's nerves were a bit frayed but she pulled herself together. Grandma, will you be my matron of honor?"

"I would be delighted, my dear."

Jennifer should have been the one walking before Megan. They dreamed about being each other's maid of honor ever since they were in grade school. Megan mourned the loss of her friend but she had a lot to thank God for.

Rose straightened up and took her position.

Chapter 28

Jackson requested to speak with his parents at the same time Megan was talking to her grandparents.

"Mom, Dad I've asked Megan to marry me."

He waited for a response but none came. His parents looked at each other and his mother said to his father, "Give me five." With that she slapped her husband in the hand. Jackson looked with surprise at both of them. His father opened his wallet and gave his mother a hundred-dollar bill.

"You win."

"What's going on?"

Your mother said that you were in love with Megan, and being the fool I am, I said no." His father laughed. "I wish you all the happiness in the world. After the hell you've been through, you deserve it."

His mother said, "She is a gorgeous young woman. If only she could lose some of that weight."

Jackson smiled. He couldn't wait to see his mother's surprised look when Megan walked down the aisle to him. He was excited, he had not seen her without the fat suit either and he couldn't wait. The guests were all asked to take their seats and the ceremony began.

Jackson and Jacob stood under the arch beaded with roses. Jacob held his father's hand while they waited. The girls came up the walkway and then Rose proudly and slowly walked down the aisle to the tune 'Here comes the bride.' And then Peter Sr. with a very slim and gorgeous Megan on his arm, walked behind Rose.

An audible gasp came from every opened mouth. Mrs. Montgomery was shocked, her dropped jaw made Jackson smile and chuckle as he winked at his mother. Joan was totally confused and completely shocked.

Marcia shook her brother, "Peter, look, that's our little Megan! We have our Megan back!" Her eyes teared up.

No one believed what they were seeing. What happened to all of that weight she gained? Everyone who saw Megan the past months knew that she had to be at least two hundred pounds. Here came this slim, elegant and very beautiful young lady they all knew and loved before her horrendous marriage to Tom.

She looked gorgeous in an elegant white gown that fell softly against her shapely body. This was Lizzie's creation. Jackson's kind and loving eyes and his smile said it all. He was the happiest man in the world. Her Grandfather took her to Jackson and stood behind them. Megan turned around to face the people she cared about and she spoke heartfelt words to them.

"Before I say my vows, I want to say a few words to all of you. I love you all and that is why you are all here. I know that many of you were surprised to see my miraculous weight loss and I'm sorry that I deceived you but it was the only way I could think of saving my life. Those of you who knew my past will understand what I'm talking about. For months I wore a fat suit. Wearing that suit literally saved my life and when I took it off today, I also shed my past. I want to thank God for giving me the idea to begin the process of deliverance and I want to thank my three faithful and loving friends for helping me to go through with this plan. She pointed to where Lulu, Lizzie and Ariel were sitting and they stood up. I'm saddened that one I considered a part of this inner circle, one that I've love most of my life is not here and has exited my life but in all fairness I must thank Jennifer for introducing me to Jackson." She blew a kiss to her friends, "Thank you guys." They all blew her a kiss and sat down. "Today I am embracing a bright future by marrying a wonderful guy and I want to start with a clean slate."

Megan turned to face Jackson and then said, "I am ready."

Jackson smiled and they faced the minister together. The minister said, "Who gives this woman to wed this man?" And Peter Sr. proudly said, "I do." and then he sat down. They said their wedding vows the traditional way. After the vows and the kiss, the minister said.

"I want to introduce to you Mr. and Mrs. Jackson Montgomery."

The guests stood to their feet and applauded as the bride and groom walked down the path carpeted with rose petals and entered the ballroom created in the middle of the garden. Speeches and toasts were made to the bride and groom by family and friends. After all ceremonies were performed, Jackson and Megan danced their first dance to the song "At Last." The band played into the wee hours of the morning while everyone danced to romantic love songs under the moonlit and star studded skies. The ocean breeze kept them cool on a hot summer's night. It was a magical evening.

Chapter 29

Megan did not want to go on a honeymoon and so Jackson planned to sleep by himself in his bedroom that night. He wanted to keep his promise not to pressure her into a sexual relationship. He was standing on the veranda outside of his bedroom enjoying the beautiful night air and reminiscing about his beautiful wedding day when he heard a knock on his door. His bride looked stunning in a black negligee, she stood before him.

"May I come in, Sir?"

He stood with an opened mouth. She panicked. *Was she too forward? What was he thinking of her?* Her memory of her wedding night with Tom surfaced. *Why won't he say anything?* Her mind whirled. A look of distress appeared on her face and Jackson realized that he was giving her the wrong impression.

"Forgive me, I was struck with your beauty and I was speechless. Come in."

She proceeded to do what she planned to do with much trepidation. She got the nerve and she dropped her gown.

Jackson moved in and gently pulled her close. He kissed her softly and then again and again.

"Are you sure you are ready? I told you I would wait."

"I'm ready."

This time he kissed her passionately. He had imagined this scene on several occasions. He wanted her badly and she wanted him. Their love was perfect. He picked her up and took her to his bed.

"My wife, my beautiful wife. I love you."

He kissed her and he ravished her body.

"I love you Jackson. I love you."

He entered her and the rhythm of their body was one. They moved in such perfect concert. And then it was over. Two satisfied lovers lay in each other's arms and fell asleep.

The next morning, Megan awoke in Jackson's arm. She panicked. A nervous Megan ran downstairs to make breakfast. Jackson turned over, and his wife was gone. He got up and went downstairs to find her. In a panicked voice, she spoke, "I was making breakfast. I was going to bring it up to you."

He was shocked at her behavior and walked over to her. As he approached her, she raised both hands anticipating to be hit. Megan's mind went back to her honeymoon with Tom. Tom was wonderful before their honeymoon. Somewhere in the deepest part of her mind, she was expecting the very same thing to happen with Jackson. He realized what was happening, and he backed away.

"Megan, please come over here."

She looked up and he was sitting down at the kitchen island. She walked over to him.

He gently pulled her close to sit in his lap. "I want you to listen to me very carefully. I am not Tom. You don't have to be my maid. Hire as many people as you want to do the work around here. You are my queen. I love you. We'll order in or I'll cook, we can cook together or we can go out. It's up to you. Now, listen.

I have never hit a woman. I have never had the desire to do so. Are we going to disagree? Yes. But I expect you to be yourself. If I am being a jerk, which I have been called before, then say so. I want us to be honest with each other. I have another suggestion," He waited and when she said nothing he continued. "What do you think about family therapy? You, me, and the children. You can redecorate the house to make it your own. Call in someone to help you."

Tears of joy streamed down her cheeks. "I am so sorry. I just had a bad moment but I'm glad I did. You are the most wonderful man in the world."

He chuckled. "I am not going to disagree with you."

"Jackson why didn't you have me sign a pre-nuptial? I would have signed one, you know."

"I know, but when I took you as my wife, I made a vow before God and before several witnesses, I promised to love you and take care of you until death. I have no plans to divorce you. I think that I need to tell you that I made the same promise to Michelle and I intend to keep it. I have set up a fund for her until her death. I would never have divorced her. The marriage was over but I made a vow to God."

"Then why did you divorce her?"

"I believe that part of loving someone is giving them what they want and I knew that she wanted her freedom. She had a lot of help from Jennifer in making up her mind."

"What did Jen have to do with it?"

"Well, I didn't tell you before because I didn't want to spoil our wedding day. After Tom left I went to visit Jennifer. I was angry with her and wanted to confront her. She went insane and she told me that she was the one who told Michelle that the best thing would be for her to leave. Jennifer was the one who drove Michelle home to her parents. In her sick mind, Jennifer thought that she and I would get married. Megan, she hates you so much. After I left, she smashed her head into a glass door and called the police and accused me of assault."

Megan turned around to face him. "What? When did all this happen? Jackson you should have told me? I'm so sorry."

"Honey, don't worry, it's all cleared up. There were witnesses to the time I visited her and she will be brought up on charges for making a false report. She is in the psych ward. I'll tell you all the details later. I just want to hold you close."

She snuggled up against him.

"Jackson, I am so sorry. Honey, I love you."

Megan had taken out the things to make breakfast and she decided to take Jackson at his word.

"Okay mister, make me breakfast."

"I most certainly will, but before your humble servant slaves away for you, I would like to ask you to do something with me."

"What my king?"

"Join me at the Throne of Grace."

Jackson knelt down behind Megan and put his arms around her embracing her and he prayed. Megan couldn't help remembering that on the day after her marriage to Tom she was regurgitating and reeling from the most horrendous experience. And here she was the day after her marriage to Jackson wrapped in his loving arms and kneeling before the Throne of Grace while he spoke heartfelt words to a loving God. He kissed her and then he got up.

"Okay, My Lady, I am ready."

Jackson dropped his robe and got naked. Wearing only an apron he fixed a breakfast fit for a king and queen.

Megan sat down waiting to be served.

"My lady, you cannot eat this breakfast unless you get naked."

She laughed and dropped her robe. They ate and went upstairs to shower and then they made love again. She lay in his arms satisfied and happy.

"I like the way you look at me, the tender way you touch me. Oh! And I really like kissing those lovely manly lips and most of all I love the way you love me."

"Really?"

"Really." Megan said, "We never talked about children, would you be interested in making some more babies? I want a noisy home with a lot of children and lots of laughter, singing, and play. I want joy and I want us to create it."

"You can have as many children as you like my dear wife, but I must insist on a lot of practice." They laughed and then he said. "But seriously, I thought that you wanted to have a career in film?"

"There was a time when I wanted a career but I would like to take some time to savor the treasures God has given to me."

He laughed a hearty laugh. "I'm a treasure? I like that. The last few months have been the best months of my adult life. Living with Michelle, I was always on edge waiting, just waiting for something to happen. I never knew how, where, when or what but something always erupted. I thank God for my parents. My mother ran this home until you came and my father ran the firm most of the time so that I could get the flexibility I needed. Mom just couldn't do it anymore. They haven't had a vacation in years. After you came our lives became normal. He kissed her forehead. "Thank you for coming into my life."

Jackson and Megan enjoyed a wonderful honeymoon right there at home.

Chapter 30

Jackson and Megan were having fun on their honeymoon but they missed the children and decided to bring them home. They got dressed and went over to his parents to get the kids. Jackson rang the doorbell and the children ran to the door.

"It's Daddy and Mommy. We can call you Mommy, right."

Megan looked to Jackson for approval.

He picked up Jacob and said, "Yes. You may." He went on into the great room where his parents were looking at television. He listened to the murder story that was being aired and he ran out to Megan. "Megan lets go"

"What wrong? Aren't we going to get the children's things?"

"No. Let's go."

"Jackson, I thought that we agreed that we were going to be honest with each other. What's wrong with your parents?"

"It's Tom. His wife murdered him. It's on the news."

"What?" She ran inside and Ariel was reporting the news.

"Dr. Brinkley was found on the living room floor in his luxurious apartment. A butcher knife stuck in his heart and several stab wounds to various parts of his body. The experts say that this was a crime of passion. His wife Denise Douglas-Brinkley was arrested.

According to the police reports, last Thursday morning Tom Brinkley returned home angry."

"Megan that's the day he attacked you."

His parents with shocked expressions on their faces, both spoke at the same time.

"Attacked, Megan he attacked you?"

"We'll tell you about it later, let's listen to Ariel's report. Jackson turned up the volume."

"Dr. Brinkley 'allegedly' chained his wife to the bed and raped and sodomized her repeatedly. According to police report, yesterday evening she begged to be free on the pretense that she wanted to fix him a special dinner. He untied her and after she cleaned herself up, she brought him a beer laced with enough sleeping pills to be lethal and when she was sure that he couldn't wake up she stabbed him to death."

Frank Dudley, the reporter in the newsroom questioned Ariel. "Ariel, what can you tell us about his wife?"

"Frank, she is from a very prominent family. The Douglas' are one of the wealthiest families in the Country. Denise Douglas lived a very privileged lifestyle, she is a world traveler and her friends and associates are High Society. This is going to be a well-publicized case and you can be sure that the best defense attorneys will be hired."

"Ariel, didn't you cover their wedding a few weeks ago?"

"Yes Frank, I did. It was an extravagant and beautiful wedding."

"Ariel will you keep us posted?

"Yes Frank, I'll keep you updated as the details become available. This is Ariel Rosenberg reporting for WJLB News Station."

Megan's cell phone rang, it was Lulu.

"Hi Lulu."

"Are you watching the news? The bastard got his just deserves. His wife was arrested for stabbing him with the biggest kitchen knife she could find and then once in the heart. Honey I'm sorry to be so happy but I believe that he wasn't finished with you. He would have found some way to finish the job. I applaud her and I'll be praying for her. Every Television station is airing stories about the Douglas family and Tom."

"The poor woman! Lulu we're at my in-laws picking up the kids. Call Ariel and Lizzie, let's get together tonight at my house. Bye."

Chapter 31

Ariel returned to the newsroom and she walked into her boss's office and slammed the door behind her.

He said, "Come in. Close my door, will you."

"I want to investigate Tom Brinkley's background. I know a lot more that I am willing to disclose at the moment but the media is telling a life story that is too perfect. I believe that there's a big story here."

"You really think so?"

"I really do."

"Then go for it, but don't waste too much time. If you don't find anything soon I'm going to have to pull the story."

"I really feel that there is a big story here. Thanks boss."

Ariel, Lizzie, and Lulu headed over to Megan's. They all sat around the kitchen island.

"Guys, I am going to Harvard to check out Tom's story. I am positive that he has a history as an abuser."

Ariel, I hope you find whatever you need to free that woman because she is a hero in my book."

"Lulu, no one deserves to die, not even Tom."

"Wrong! He did! And he deserved to die exactly the way she did it."

"Lulu, I didn't like him either, but he was a human being."

"Lizzie, I am not having this conversation with you. I will never change my mind so let's drop it."

Megan was getting a headache.

"Lizzie and Lulu stop."

"Megan, did you tell Ariel about Jen?"

"Lulu, I was just about to ask what happened. Megan, I heard what you said about Jen at the wedding. I didn't understand and I have been meaning to ask you about it. Unfortunately I got very busy, and truthfully, I forgot."

Lizzie with a distress look on her face answered, "She's not a part of this group anymore. I can't believe that we were friends since kindergarten and I really didn't know Jen. I would never have believed what she did if I hadn't seen for myself."

"What did she do?" asked Ariel.

Lulu told Ariel everything Jennifer did. A shocked and disappointed Ariel said, Wow! Jen, I don't know what to say. Is anyone going to see her?"

Lulu said, "Hell no!"

But Megan said, "Lulu I've been thinking about it. I love Jen and I know that she is hurting because she believes that I took Jackson from her, but I don't know what to say to her."

Lulu turned around to face Megan square in the face. "No! Don't even bother! Megan she confessed to me that she was the one who sent you the picture and the roses and she caused your car accident! She almost killed you."

"What?" Megan could not believe what she was hearing. "I knew that she went to Tom and she accused Jackson of attacking her but I had no idea that she was behind those dreadful pranks."

Lulu said, "Well, she was and she confessed to me."

Ariel and Lizzie looked at each other and they both said, "What are you talking about?"

Lulu explained. "Well, we didn't want to worry anyone so we kept quiet. Megan received a very disturbing picture of a rag doll hanging from a noose and at the bottom scrawled in blood was her name. Then she received a box of dead black flowers and a note that said that the flowers were dead just like her. Her car brakes were tampered with causing an accident, but thank God that she ran into a bush and wasn't hurt. I knew that wasn't Tom style and I noticed Jennifer's attitude towards Megan, I saw that green eyed monster in her. So I suspected that it was Jennifer but I had no proof. It wasn't by accident that I was at the restaurant when she met with Tom, I followed her there. When we visited her at the hospital and Lizzie left, I confronted her and made her confess."

"Oh my God. Poor Jen, she is a sick soul."

Lulu had it with Lizzie.

"Lizzie stop, I've had it with your holy pity or whatever it is you think that you are feeling. Jennifer was not a nice person and no one saw it."

Hurt and shocked they all sat quietly mulling things over, but although they knew what Jennifer was capable of, they still didn't want to believe that she was that lost. Tears flowed down each face, Megan, Lizzie and Ariel shared the pain of losing not only a dear friend but a close sister. They loved her and hoped and prayed for her recovery. They sat around the rest of the evening reminiscing and comforting each other, but it was a solemn night.

The trial was set to begin in a few weeks. Megan and everyone in the town followed the news reports closely. Denise Douglas Brinkley was being painted in the Media as the evil jealous wife who lost her temper and killed her husband. Time passed quickly

Chapter 32

Ariel went to Harvard Medical school admissions office and found out that Tom did attend school there but he was on a full scholarship. His records showed that he was not from Boston he was from Nevada. She called her office and spoke to her boss and told him that she was going to Tom's hometown in Nevada.

Ariel flew to Nevada and checked into a hotel on Main Street. She could not find the Brinkley family. No one knew them. Everywhere she turned, she met a brick wall. Maybe there was nothing there, but something in her gut told her that there was. A week passed and her boss was not going to waste time and money, so he told her that she was to return to the office the next day.

There was a nice restaurant at the corner of 8th Avenue that she wanted to try. The hotel concierge recommended the restaurant and Ariel decided to eat dinner there. She planned to return to the hotel after dinner, call her husband, get a good night's sleep and get an early start.

As Ariel walked down Main Street, she noticed the brothels and her curiosity peaked. They were legal in this state and men boldly entered and exited those doors. She was in deep thought when her attention was drawn to the big bold letters on one of the brothels; the address was 2680 Houston Street. That was the address on Tom's admission records. She went into the building to inquire, but no one knew the Brinkleys'. She was back to where she started, but then she noticed the Madam had a strong resemblance to Tom and decided to play a hunch. She walked up to her, smiling, she said, "Excuse me but you look very familiar, I have a friend and I could swear that you are related to him."

"Oh really, what is his name?"

"Tom, He went to Harvard Medical School."

"That's odd, my son Tom went to Harvard and he's a doctor."

"For the life of me I can't remember his last name, it's been so long."

"Tom Bronson but he changed it when he got away from this God forsaken place."

"Really, this isn't such a bad place to grow up, is it?"

"You don't know the half of it."

"Why don't you tell me?"

Ariel got her speaking and when she was finished she called her boss and arranged for her camera crew to be flown up. The crew left immediately and would arrive later that night. Ariel went back to the hotel and then she called home.

Her husband answered. "Hi honey, when are you coming back? I miss you."

"David, this story is big. You won't believe what I have discovered. I'll be back before you know it. I love you."

"I love you too. Bye."

The newsroom buzzed with excitement of the upcoming interview and her boss was happy that this big story was his. The crew was set up and ready for her interviews.

The trial was slated on the dockets to begin on Monday.

It was a beautiful Saturday afternoon two days before the trial and the kids were at their grandparents. Jackson and Megan sat around the swimming pool that overlooked the ocean.

"What an intoxicating view! It takes my breath away! I remember the day the realtor brought me here. The landscaping was awesome. The magnificent gardens, the flowers and the foliage bursting with rich color caught my attention but when I saw this view, I said this is it and bought this property immediately."

"What do you think of when you stand out here in the mornings drinking your coffee?"

"Before you came along I wished for a normal life. Now I think about you and feel blessed. That is why I want to do something to help others.

"What do you want to do?"

"I have a few ideas mulling around in my head but when I get it together I would like it to be a family project. Will you join me?"

"Aye. Aye. Sir. I work one day a week at the shelter for battered women and I would like to expand that by speaking out against domestic abuse."

Jackson was impressed. He said, "I think that is a wonderful idea and I'll back you up with whatever you need."

"Oh! Thank you honey. Jackson I want to go to the trial. I want to be there for her."

"Why would you want to put yourself through that?"

"Jackson you just mentioned that you want to help others. I want to help her, if I can. I feel the need to be there. I spoke to Lulu and Lizzie about it and they said that they would go with me. We haven't been able to get in touch with Ariel."

"I'll go with you."

"You don't have to. You do so much for me. I'll be fine knowing that you and the kids are here when I come home."

"That's sweet but I am going to go with you and be there for you. No arguments."

"What about the office."

"If the boss can't take time off, who can? Dad will cover me."

———— ◉ ————

Megan was eight weeks pregnant and she was truly enjoying life to the fullest. Family therapy was a good idea, they were making great progress and she had also taken on the project of remodeling her new home.

Chapter 33

The day of the trial arrived. A crowd gathered outside the courthouse and the courtroom was filled to capacity. The towns people, rich and poor alike were there. Television reporters filed in. Denise Douglas-Brinkley was brought in. She was a very attractive woman dressed in a black tailored Versace suit and her stocking feet wore Manolo Blahnik high heels. Her blonde hair was pulled back in a tight bun and her makeup was expertly done. She sat next to her two power attorneys and her parents were seated in the first row behind the defense team.

"All rise! The honorable Monica Ramsey presiding."

The judge entered the courtroom. She was a very attractive black woman. Her skin shone in its richness. Her short cropped haircut looked stylish and elegant. Her makeup was subtle but well done and her nails were professionally manicured. Her essence and decorum told you who she was.

"Everyone may be seated." The Clerk read the docket. "The case of the State Of North Carolina vs Denise Douglas-Brinkley. The charge is murder in the first degree. The prosecutor will give his opening statement."

The prosecutor confidently strolled over to where the members of the jury were seated. He stopped and looked at each person in the eye and then he proceeded to speak.

"Ladies and gentlemen of the jury the prosecution will show that Denise Brinkley maliciously and with pre-meditation killed her husband. We will show that Denise Brinkley is a spoiled rich, controlling, possessive woman who always gets what she wants and in a jealous fit of rage she killed her husband. Thank you."

He bowed and walked back to his seat and the clerk said, "The defense will now make their opening remarks." The defense attorney got up. He looked in the direction of the prosecution and then he smiled. He walked over to the Jury and after viewing each face he spoke deliberately and calmly.

"Ladies and gentlemen, it is the prosecution's duty to prove beyond a reasonable doubt their claims against Denise Brinkley. However the defense will prove that Denise Douglas-Brinkley was a battered woman and she killed her abuser while in a state of temporary insanity. This woman was taken to Paris on her honeymoon and her romantic dream was shattered. It was turned into a nightmare. She was kicked in her ribs, breaking two of them. She was sodomized, and called the most degrading names by the man who claimed to love her. Denise Brinkley entered this marriage with the expectation of a loving relationship with the wonderful man who courted her but instead she encountered an unrecognizable Dr. Jekyll and Mr. Hyde."

Gregory Thompson turned and walked back to his seat beside the defendant.

The clerk said, "The prosecution will call its first witness."

The prosecutor stood to his feet, looked at his notepad, and said, "We call Iris Watley to the stand."

Iris walked pass Denise and scowled as she took her seat. The clerk held the Bible and Iris placed her right hand on the Bible and raised her left hand.

"Do you swear to tell the truth, the whole truth, and nothing but the truth?"

"I do."

"Mrs. Watley would you please state your full name for the court?"

"My name is Iris Watley."

"Mrs. Watley what was your relationship to the victim?"

"I am an OR nurse and Dr. Brinkley was one of the anesthesiologists who worked in the OR."

"How would you describe him?"

"He was a very nice man. He was kind and thoughtful. He took excellent care of his patients. He checked and rechecked to see how his patients were doing. It was a pleasure to work with him."

"Do you think that Dr. Brinkley was an abuser?"

"No."

"Do you know Denise Brinkley?"

"Yes, she is a nurse supervisor on the fifth floor."

"What was your relationship with her?"

"I didn't have a relationship with her. I tried not to have anything to do with her."

"And why is that?"

"She was very demanding and rude."

"Would you say that she is hot tempered?"

"I would say that she is rude and demanding."

"Would you say that she would easily lose control?"

"Yes, especially if things weren't going her way."

"Thank you."

All the character witnesses said the same thing. It was Denise Brinkley's word against the evidence.

The defense didn't have much of a case. There were no visible bruises or evidence that she was beaten. By the third day things were looking very bad for Denise Brinkley. Her Attorneys were getting frustrated. The prosecutor called their last witness. Tom's boss was sworn in.

"Doctor, you were Tom Brinkley's boss, were you not."

"Yes. I was."

"Would you please describe the deceased?"

"Yes. He was a very nice guy, easy to work with and a very hard worker. He was a private person. My only contact with him was at the hospital."

"Did he ever at any time display uncontrolled anger that you can recall?"

"No! Never!"

"Your Honor, the prosecution rests."

Everyone who spoke for the prosecution had the same testimony. Tom was a good guy.

The judge said, "Due to the lateness of the hour court will recess and reconvene 8 a.m. tomorrow morning and the defense will present their case."

That night the defense tried to find Tom's friend but he was nowhere to be seen and they knew that the prosecution was going to destroy the credibility of their only witness, but her testimony was all they had.

<hr>

The next morning, court reconvened and the defense called their only witness.

"The defense calls Susan Crevell to the stand."

"Your Honor the prosecution was not informed of this witness."

"Your honor the defense was unable to contact the witness until late last night."

"I will allow the witness to testify."

Susan Crevell was sworn in.

"Ms. Crevall would you tell the court in your own words how you knew the deceased and what was your relationship to him."

"I met Tom Brinkley at a party. He was a college student at the time. The party was boring and later that night we decided to go to his apartment. He was a very nice guy at first and then, I don't quite remember what happened, I just remembered the first blow and then I awoke hours later in an alley bruised and badly beaten."

"Do you remember how you got there?"

"No."

"Tell us what happened after that. Did you go to a hospital? What happened?"

"They were afraid and thought that I had died, that is why they dumped me in the alley. His friend, I believe his name was Mike, came back just when I regained consciousness and he said that he would help me. He took me home and he took care of me until I was better. He begged me not to make trouble for Tom and he promised to make sure that Tom never bothered me again."

"Ladies and gentlemen of the Jury. Tom Brinkley was not only an abuser he would have eventually killed someone had he gotten the opportunity."

"Your Honor, we object. The victim is not on trial here!"

"Over ruled."

"Your witness."

The prosecutor began to question the witness. "Ms. Crevell, You met a man at a party and went with him back to his apartment. A man you knew nothing about."

"Yes"

"Were you drinking?"

"We had a few drinks."

"You were intoxicated and as you yourself stated, you displayed very poor judgment. Ms Crevell, you want this jury and everyone in this courtroom to believe that Tom Brinkley, a man you didn't know, beat you near death and you felt sorry for him and did not have him arrested?"

"Yes. That is what happened."

"You didn't go to the hospital, you didn't make a police report. The only witness you have to this attack is his friend. Ms. Crevell, can you tell me where this friend is, and what is his last name? We would really like to get to the bottom of this."

"I don't know where he is and I don't remember his last name."

"You don't know where he is and you don't remember his last name? The witness is excused. No more questions."

The defense was worried. They tried but couldn't find Mike Blackburn. He quit his job and left without a trace. Their only recourse was to call the defendant.

"Your Honor we would like a brief recess to speak with our client."

"There will be a twenty minute recess."

The defense attorneys and their client went into a holding room at the courthouse.

"We're going to have to put you on the stand, Denise. It's risky but we have nothing else to go on. This man has covered his tracks well and the only person who could tell us who he really was, is nowhere to be found. Putting you on the witness stand is the only chance we have of convincing the Jury."

Twenty minutes later court reconvened.

"The defense calls the defendant to the stand."

Denise Brinkley looked frail. This vibrant sophisticated woman looked weak and hopeless. This trial was surely taking its toll on her. When she stood up she almost lost her balance but she managed to pull herself together and walk with dignity to the witness stand.

"Mrs. Brinkley do you swear to tell the whole truth and nothing but the truth so help you God."

"I do."

"Would you please state your full name for the court?"

"My name is Denise Douglas-Brinkley."

"In your own words tell us about your honeymoon and the few weeks leading up to your husband's death."

"It was a living hell. My husband did not want to leave any marks on my skin because he knew that my father would destroy him professionally, so he found other ways to torment me."

She described in detail the abuse she suffered at the hand of the man she loved. She cried and could barely speak at times. She was a very believable witness.

"No more questions Your Honor."

"Would the prosecution like to cross-examine the witness?"

"Yes Your Honor."

"Mrs. Brinkley, how did you meet your husband?"

"We worked together at the hospital and we became friends. He and his wife were separated and he was very broken up about it, so I would encourage him to hang in there."

"What did he say was the cause of the separation?"

"He said that his wife stopped caring and she began to use

drugs and she gained over two hundred pounds. The marriage became unbearable and he left."

"How was the relationship between the two of you?"

"He was very romantic. He sent me flowers and he took me to the opera. On our days off we would fly into New York for dinner and Broadway shows. We had a wonderful romance."

"Your wedding was the event of the year, wasn't it? As a matter of fact we have a clip of you and your late husband having a jovial time."

The prosecution showed a tape of her and Tom dancing to romantic songs and having a merry time. They looked very happy.

"Yes, we had a very big wedding."

"And then what happened?"

She described again in detail the abuse she got at the hand of her husband.

"Mrs. Brinkley, you expect the very intelligent men and women of this jury to believe that Dr. Brinkley, a man who grew up in one of the most wealthy families, a man who attended the best schools money can afford, a well respected man by all who knew him, suddenly changed into the monster you described, overnight?"

"That's exactly what happened."

"Mrs. Brinkley you said that you were beaten, did you go to a hospital?

"Yes I did go."

He was surprised at her answer but he had to go with it.

"And what happened?"

"I told them that I fell down. I was afraid of Tom and I told them what he wanted me to say."

"You lied?"

She looked at her attorneys and she did not answer.

"Mrs. Brinkley, I asked you if you lied?"

The defense attorney said, "Your honor the prosecution is badgering the witness."

"Over ruled, the Witness will answer the question."

"Yes"

"Mrs. Brinkley would you please speak up?"

"Yes, I lied!"

"How do we know that you're not lying now?"

"Because I am telling you the truth. I lied because I was afraid of Tom."

"You lied because you were afraid of your husband and now you are lying because you are afraid of going to prison. Isn't that right?"

She looked nervous and confused.

"No"

"No what? No, you are not afraid of going to prison or 'no' you weren't afraid of your husband? Mrs. Brinkley make up your mind."

She was close to tears.

"Mrs. Brinkley, I am sure that the staff at the hospital believed you when you lied just like you are asking us to do now. No more questions."

The judge looked at the clock. It was 2:30 and it was a grueling day.

"This court will take a short recess and return in half an hour and Mr. Johnson we are going to wrap this case up."

The defense had no other witnesses and the prosecution knew it. After court was dismissed, the defense attorneys agreed to meet with the prosecutors, Ronald Gleason and Paula Gibbins. They made the same offer as before.

"The plea bargain is still open. We offer fifteen to life. She'll be out in ten for good behavior. Best offer we can make."

"Ron you know that she wouldn't survive a month in that place."

"She is guilty!

"We know, but you have to prove that she was in her right mind and that it was premeditated murder."

Ronald Gleason became agitated and he paced as he spoke. "Do you think the Jury will believe that temporary insanity crap?"

The defense attorney, Gregory Thompson felt that the prosecution knew something he didn't and was eager to win this case by pressing the issue of the plea bargain. He didn't know what to do. He needed time to think this through.

"Let me discuss your offer with my client and I'll get back to you. However, I can tell you right now, I have a feeling she will want to take her chances with the Jury "

The recess ended and they were back in court. Everyone was seated.

Just then the clerk gave Megan's note to the defense attorney. He read it and then he said,

"Your Honor new evidence has come to my attention and I am asking for the leniency of the court. I am requesting a continuance."

"Your Honor, I object. This is ludicrous. The defense is stalling for time. This is a waste of taxpayers' dollars."

The Judge was annoyed. "It's wonderful to know that the prosecution is concerned about the taxpayers, but a woman's life is at stake here. I will allow it. Mr. Johnson this had better be good. You have until 8 a.m. tomorrow morning. Court is in recess."

The reporters hovered around the courthouse to find out what the new evidence was.

Chapter 34

Megan walked over to the Douglas' and introduced herself and she smiled at the shocked look on Denise's face. From her testimony she was expecting to see a 300-pound whale that was on drugs. Megan got close to her ear and whispered,

"He lied."

The defense attorneys, Denise, her parents and Megan went into an office in the courthouse.

"Mrs. Brinkley I hope you have something substantial that we could use because as we stand, our client is doomed."

"It's Mrs. Montgomery."

"Sorry, but Mrs. Montgomery I mean it. We need a miracle."

"I might just have that, Mr. Johnson. Put me on the stand and let me tell my story I believe that I will be able to help your client. I too suffered abuse from that beast and I have proof."

"Okay. You are all that we have."

"And I am all that you need. Oh! I have a request, could you arrange for a television and a DVD player."

"What?"

"Trust me."

"Well, we could use the one the prosecution used today."

"Good, see you in the morning."

Megan rejoined her husband and friends. Lulu and Lizzie followed Jackson as he drove home. As Jackson drove he began to speak.

"Megan, what is going on?"

"Jackson, I am going to help to free that woman."

"Megan, I am worried about you. You are pregnant and God knows you have gone through enough."

"I am blessed to have you and the kids. I couldn't live with myself if I didn't do my best to help Denise. She is me. At least that is who I was. If God did not help me, I probably would be in her shoes or dead."

"I am going to be right there with you honey"

"Jackson, I don't want you to see what I'm about to show the court. Please don't come. I don't want you to see how weak I was."

"I won't come if you don't want me to, but I can imagine."

"Stay at home. Please."

"As you wish, but I want you to let my mother go with you. She loves you, you know."

"I know. I will ask your mother to go with me."

"Then it's settled."

They arrived home, ate dinner, and eagerly sat in front of the television waiting for Ariel's report.

The six o'clock news came on and everyone was captivated. They could not get enough of the trial. Janet Jones and Frank Dudley reported on the events of the day in court and made comments.

"Janet, it was a rough day in court for Denise Brinkley. The prosecution destroyed her testimony. It looks real bad for her."

"Frank, if what she says is true Tom Brinkley was really a monster and it would be a travesty if she was abused the way she said and then have to pay such a heavy penalty."

"My sources tell me that his ex-wife will be testifying for the defense tomorrow morning. Janet, we also have a special report." He looked straight at the camera. "And now we have a special report from Ariel Rosenberg in Nevada. Ariel, you have been in Nevada investigating Tom Brinkley. Can you tell us what you found out?"

"Yes, Frank. I went to Harvard Medical School and I found out that Tom Brinkley did attend that University but he went there on a scholarship. He was not from a wealthy family in Boston. I got on the next plane and here I am. Well, what I found out is shocking. Tom grew up in this city and he lived in this building."

Ariel stood in front of the building and she pointed to the sign in big bold letters.

"It's the brothel Tom's mother runs. His last name is not Brinkley and the web of lies he spun I'm about to untangle."

Megan looked at Jackson in disbelief. She might not have been legally married to Tom. Lulu drew his chair closer and Lizzie held his hand almost squeezing it. Frank, the reporter continued, "Wow! No one suspected that he was a fraud?"

"No, Frank. He did a good job deceiving everyone."

"Did you interview his family and friends?"

"Yes, Frank. A few people I interviewed said that he was a nice guy but many people were reluctant to comment.

I found out that Tom dated a beautiful debutant and her parents did not like him at all. They thought that he was not good enough for their daughter and openly rejected him. They forbade their daughter from seeing him. One week later the entire family was stabbed to death and their home was burned to the ground. Tom was a person of interest in that case but his mother and her employees gave him an airtight alibi. The case was never solved and Tom left the State of Nevada, changed his name and never returned.

"My God!"

"Lulu, be quiet." Said Lizzie

Ariel was still speaking.

"It was also rumored but not proven that before he left, he raped and assaulted two of his mother's employees and that she kept things quiet."

"Ariel, everyone who has testified is saying that he was a nice guy."

Lulu said, "Nice guy, my ass!"

"Lulu, please!"

Lizzie was listening intently and wanted Lulu to be quiet. Frank was still talking.

"The defense is having a very difficult time. What about his family? Did you talk to them?"

"Frank, I want you to hear what his mother had to say. This is the interview I had with Helen Bronson, Tom's mother."

Helen Bronson was a brunette about 5'6' and about 175 lbs. She had a raspy voice and was a chain smoker. Anyone could see that she was a good looking woman in her youth who hadn't learned to dress appropriately for her age.

Lulu laughed. "With a mother like that, no wonder he hates women!"

"Ms. Bronson, How long have you been running this brothel?"

"Oh! Since my boy was about five. I would say about thirty years."

"Ms. Bronson, you told me that you never married."

"Well, yes. I never got married and Tom grew up without a father but my boy was a good boy."

"Did Tom know his father?"

"No, he didn't, but he was proud of who he was, and he was very smart. Because of me and what I do, those rich people looked down their noses on my boy. He hated them and this place and couldn't wait to get as far away as possible. I'm not surprised that he changed his name. It's not a crime to change your name, is it?"

"No, Ma'am. Ms. Bronson, you had no idea where your son went when he left Harvard, did you?"

"No."

"Don't you think that was strange?"

"We weren't that close and he hated this place. I didn't expect to see or hear from him, but I never thought that I would be hearing of his murder."

"Ms. Bronson, what about the rumors that Tom assaulted your employees?"

"Lies, I tell you, all lies."

Lulu was angry, "What a bitch! She and her son are a pair from hell. She covered up for him the same way your mother did."

Megan kept quiet and Jackson kept his eyes on her, but he understood how Lulu felt.

"Ms. Bronson, I am very sorry to be the bearer of bad news. When I approached you I thought that you knew that Tom had passed. I am very sorry for your loss, please accept my condolences."

"Thank you. I hope that wife of his get what she deserves."

Lulu was really upset and he said, "No, she didn't. Megan, you have to help that woman. She can't go to prison for that scum bag."

"Ms. Bronson, thank you for your time. And now Frank, back to you."

"Ariel, so what now?"

"Frank, I don't know. We know that Tom Brinkley was not who he claimed to be. It seems that he was not the nice guy he portrayed."

"Well Ariel, we understand that the defense is depending on his ex-wife, she is to testify tomorrow."

Ariel looked a bit shocked but she kept her composure. She had to call Megan when she went off the air.

"Frank, if anyone can help I believe that she can. Our prayers are with Denise Brinkley."

"So Ariel, what now?"

"Frank, I'll be on my way home as soon as I wrap things up here. Tomorrow I'll be in court covering the case."

"Safe trip."

Lulu and Lizzie realized that Megan needed some time alone and they decided to leave.

Lulu said to Megan, "Honey, we'll be there first thing in the morning." They hugged and kissed and left.

———◦《◦》◦———

Joan's jaw dropped in disbelief and total embarrassment. Tom had made a fool of her. "Oh my God! Tom! What the hell? I don't believe this!"

Peter threw his head back and had a good laugh at her. "There is your physician, from Boston. He is *OLD MONEY*, you say." He laughed again "I'm sure that the Johns who frequent his mother's brothel have *OLD MONEY*. He laughed again and walked away.

The phones of all who knew Tom lit up. They were all shocked at what they had just heard. The televisions in public places were on and every television station buzzed with the new information. Psychiatrist, legal experts, everyone was weighing in on the events of the trial. The defense still needed *Megan*. Tom was a suspect in a murder and arson case but he was not arrested or convicted. He changed his name and lied about where he came from but that did not prove that his murder wasn't cold blooded and premeditated. He was certainly the victim here.

Chapter 35

Early the next morning the crowd filed into the courtyard and the surrounding area. Reporters were everywhere, they were trying to get a glimpse of Megan and get her comments.

Megan, dressed in one of Lizzie's originals that fit her slim body perfectly walked up the steps to the courtroom. She stopped to speak with Ariel but didn't give any information on her testimony for the public to hear. She was accompanied by her mother-in-law, Lulu and Lizzie, her parents, grandparents, and Aunt Marcia were also there. Megan was called to the stand and sworn in.

"Mrs. Montgomery, were you married to the deceased?"

"Yes."

"Were you ever on drugs?"

"No! Never!"

"And I can see that you are not three hundred pounds."

Everyone laughed.

"Why did Dr. Brinkley divorce you?"

Megan turned to the judge. "Your Honor, I am here because I know that Denise Brinkley is telling the truth. I would like to ask the court's indulgence. I have heard it said that a picture is worth a thousand words. I have with me a few tapes. Before I married

Tom, he was the most wonderful man in the world and I thought that I was the luckiest woman in the world. I am a photographer and I wanted to surprise my husband with a tape of our wedding night. I secretly set up cameras in our hotel suite and planned to turn them off when we made love but I was the one surprised. What I captured on these films is inexplicable. No one would ever believe without seeing."

"Let's see the evidence." The judge spoke to the Bailiff. "Bradley would you please put the tapes into the DVD player so that we could view the evidence that has now become available."

"Yes, Your Honor."

While Bradley placed the tape in the DVD player Megan spoke.

"Your Honor, I have to warn you that what you are about to see is not only evil, it is also vulgar and disgusting."

She smiled and said, "I can handle it."

The court reviewed the tapes of abuse and after each tape the people in the courtroom were tearful, angry and disgusted. The tape of him asking Joan for her help the night he almost killed her daughter, was the one that shocked the entire courtroom. They all listened intently to their conversation and Joan's responses drew the breath of everyone.

When he urinated in her face and she rose up. Everyone in the courtroom cried out. When it was over there was not a dry eye in the courtroom. There was silence. A long moment of silence. The judge picked up the stack of papers on her desk, fixed them, and put them back down in front of her. She lifted her tear stained face. The Bailiff provided her with tissues. She wiped her tears away and she slowly shook her head in disbelief and then she said,

"He made you sleep naked? He became offended if you got dressed for bed?

He kept you naked and vulnerable so that he could rape you in the middle of the night over and over and then kick you out of bed when he was finished. Naked!" She was angry now. Through gritted teeth she said, "But when he urinated on you his intention was to strip you of the last little bit of dignity you had. What a monster! Where is your mother? I think I recognize her from the film. Council, we are going to take a short recess, both of you, and the immediate Garrison family in my chambers, now!"

The reporters ran outside to get their reports on the news. This was big.

Judge Ramsey stormed into her chambers and waited impatiently for them. She loosened up her gown and then she leaned against her desk. Through gritted teeth she said. "Mrs. Garrison what in God's Heavenly name were you thinking? How could you love that monster we just witnessed more than your own child?"

Joan's response was, "Your Honor, he was not perfect but he was nice to me. He treated me with respect and honor…"

"Respect? And Honor? I can't believe that you would use those words in the very same sentence with this monster. Mrs. Garrison, You look sophisticated, very tailored and you are obviously a very beautiful woman. From your speech I gather that you are an intelligent human being. Please don't insult me. The moment he touched your daughter, he *DISRESPECTED YOU AND YOUR ENTIRE FAMILY!* You say that he treated you with respect and honor, how would you describe his treatment of his wife. Your only child. This wasn't about you! You weren't being beaten on a daily basis! Now in the scene when he thought that he almost killed your baby, your little girl, you showed no concern for her! Your only concern was to help him from being found out by his colleagues. He *DUMPED* your beaten and pregnant child in your living room and left her, and you, cleaned up his mess, protecting him all the way."

"Your Honor, I wasn't thinking clearly. Until I saw those tapes today, I didn't understand the extent of the abuse Megan suffered. I am sorry."

"You owe me no apology but the person you need to apologize to is your daughter.

"And Mr. Garrison," She shook her head in disbelief. "You sat at the table in this man's apartment when he had just finished beating your daughter. She sat across from you and your wife. She was bruised. Black eyed, swollen lips, black and blue face and arms and you bowed your head and ate and drank wine and made polite conversation while your wife acted as if Megan was not even in the room. Who does that!? What kind of people would do that to their child!? I have seen some pretty unbelievable things in my career as a judge but this beats all."

"Your Honor, like my wife said, we had an idea of what was going on. We didn't understand the frequency and the extent of the abuse she was suffering."

"Mr. Garrison, the first hint of abuse should have sent both of you reeling! You didn't protect your child. There is no excuse for that. By the way, Megan, you did a phenomenal job. Are you a professional cinematographer?"

"Yes, Your Honor, I studied cinematography at Princeton."

"Princeton! I just can't imagine growing up in a home with parents like the two of you. How did the two of you manage to have such a beautiful, obviously intelligent, and loving offspring?" The Judge stopped for a moment as her childhood memories flooded her mind and a tear trickled down her cheek. She gritted her teeth again and choked up with emotion she spoke. "My grandfather referred to me as the black one. He would never call me by my name, *EVER*, when I graduated from law school he told his friends that his grand-daughter was a lawyer. When his friends asked which one, he said, the black one. My parents covered me, they recognized the effect that his words had and they corrected him every time. Every time he did it. He never stopped and they never let him get away with it. Mrs. Garrison, I know the generation that you were spawned from. A generation of Blacks who were taught to hate themselves. You need to take a good look at yourself. You should thank God for the blessing he gave to you in Megan."

"Your Honor, we are really sorry."

"Mr. Garrison, as I have told your wife, don't apologize to me, you should be apologizing to Megan."

"We will, Your Honor, we will."

The prosecutor spoke.

"Your Honor, The Garrison's or the deceased are not on trial."

"No! Mr. Gleason, but they should be. I am finished here."

"Your Honor, may I speak."

"Sure, Megan, go ahead."

"Your Honor, in defense of my parents, they weren't nurturing. There were no hugs and kisses from them, but they weren't that bad. They worked hard and were gone a lot but my mother taught me discipline. She instilled in me the importance of a good education and she made sure that I had the best that money could afford. It was alright because when I needed to be loved I went to my grandparents and my aunt." There was a warm smile on Megan's face. "My Aunt Marcia would let me pretend that she was my mother and we would cuddle, and she told me stories. She took me to the movies and to all the fun places kids like. My fondest and most loving childhood memories are about the times spent with my father's family. They provided the love I needed and brought balance into my life. Your Honor, the abuse started with Tom."

"Mr. and Mrs. Garrison, as I said before, Megan is an exceptional loving and warm, young lady and you should be very proud of her."

They both said, "We are, Your Honor."

The Judge said, "We will return to the courtroom."

They left the Judge's chambers and returned to the courtroom. A few minutes later the Judge entered. Everyone stood up and was seated again. Joan was present in the courtroom but her mind strayed, the activity around her faded into the background. Joan was in denial until she saw the hard evidence on those films. Each man her mother dated passed before her mind and the mental and verbal abuse they caused. She and each one of her brothers had a different father. Men who entered her mother's life for a brief period of time and then left permanently. Their eyes told of their intention. She could look into their eyes and know that they wanted to rape her and she had the wisdom to protect herself. But Tom fooled her. She didn't want to see that behind those deep blue ice-cold eyes was a dark horrific world that no one else knew existed. The Judge's voice reminded her where she was.

"I will now turn this case over to the jury. You were told that this case had to be proven beyond reasonable doubt to get the full penalty. You know that the defendant did commit the crime. You are to prove that she did it with malice and that this was a premeditated act. The defense contends that their client was temporarily insane. You have seen the evidence and I hope that you will be able to come back with a fair and just verdict. "

Megan, her family, and her friends, went to lunch while the Jury deliberated. She spent most of her time on her phone. The reporters made their reports to the newspapers and television. Everyone was called back to court and Megan noticed that a few people she had invited had arrived just in time to hear the verdict. The Jury returned in two hours and everyone was called back to court.,

"Will the defendant please stand? What say ye?"

"We find the defendant, not guilty on all counts."

"Mrs. Brinkley you have been found not guilty. No one should ever take another's life. I cannot let you go free without some consequences. So I am going to sentence you to one year of house arrest and I want you to use your influence to help other women who are going through what you have experienced. You should be ever grateful to Mrs. Montgomery and the next time you find a husband, investigate him first. You can afford to do so. This case is dismissed."

Denise and her parents thanked Megan and Megan made plans to visit Denise. She liked her and wanted to be involved in helping other abused women.

The phones at the mansion were already ringing everyone wanted to interview Megan but she had already promised Ariel an exclusive.

Chapter 36

Mrs. Montgomery Sr. walked over to her daughter-in-law. "My dear I thought that Jackson went through hell but his life was a bed of roses compared to yours." She hugged Megan. "I am so sorry for what you went through, but from now on only good things will happen to you. We are going to be kind to each other and we are going to take very good care of you."

Peter and Joan stood by the door talking to each other. Joan looked at her husband and said, "Peter, you are the only constant in my life and you love me unconditionally. Even when I withdrew my love and affection from you, you stayed. Peter, what would I do without you? I know that people think of you as weak but you are my strength."

He smiled and put his arms around his wife. When Megan and her mother-in-law approached them, Joan said, "Megan, I'm sorry. I really am. I needed to see those tapes to realize what was done to you. Like you said, a picture is worth a thousand words. What can I do to make things up to you?"

"Mama, it's over. Let's forget it. My life is wonderful, I couldn't wish for a better life."

Tears were streaming down Joan's face. She held Megan's hand, and looking into her eyes she said, "Megan, I've always admired you. I wished I had your personality and intelligence. You are a beautiful…" She stopped and she smiled lovingly at her daughter and then she finished the sentence. "You are a beautiful young BLACK woman and I love you. I don't think I ever said it, but I do love you."

"Mama, I love you too. I really do."

They both had tears in their eyes.

"Mama, I have a surprise for you."

Joan wondered what it could be. The only thing Megan carried in her hands was her handbag. Megan held her mother's hand and led her over to the people she invited. They were sitting in the courtroom. Joan had noticed them sitting there and she wondered why they only came for the verdict, but later dismissed it.

"Mama, I want you to meet one of our Attorney General's and his wife."

Joan shook their hands and waited for the next introductions all the while wondering what was the point.

"And this is one of our senator's and his wife. This is the Dean of Students at one of our colleges and his wife, and this is the owner of a chain of dry cleaners."

Megan looked to see if Joan recognized any of these people but the puzzled look on her face told Megan that she didn't. Megan was amused and she smiled and said,

"Mama, these are your brothers and their wives. Jackson found them."

Joan's knees became weak and her brothers held her up.

"Oh my God!" She wept with joy. She now realized why Megan did not tell her the last names of the people she was introducing to her. She would have recognized it. When Joan could compose herself she said, "I feel ashamed. I don't know if you all will believe this, but I thought of you often and wondered what happened to you. I am so very happy to see all of you."

Megan said, "Come on, come on, this is not the place, I am inviting everyone over to my home. Jackson is barbecuing."

They piled into their cars and followed Megan home. When they arrived Megan felt that she had better warn her mother of the other surprise she had inside the house for her. "Mama, your mother is inside."

Joan's face changed and she angrily said, "I'm not ready for that."

"Mama, please! You have to resolve this. Whatever it is. If I can forgive you, you can forgive her."

"Megan, this is none of your business, you should not have done this. You had no right. Why?"

"Mama, I wanted to know why you hated yourself so much that you were willing to accept Tom and everything he represented. I realized that forcing me to marry Tom was not about me, it was about you and how you feel about being you. I had to find out what would make anyone feel that way."

"And did you find out?"

"After meeting your mother, I found out enough to do this. Come on, let's go."

Joan stood outside and she lingered.

"Mama, come on Grandma has been waiting. I didn't let her come to the courthouse because the two of you needed to meet in private."

Joan walked through the front door and her mother was standing there waiting anxiously.

"Honey, you look so good! Come on give your Mama a hug!"

Before Joan could move Mavis grabbed her and hugged her. "You smell so good."

Mavis wept on Joan's shoulder.

Joan was angry. This woman treated her like shit and now she was hugging, kissing, and crying on her? *What the hell?* Joan pushed her away.

"Mama, you were so evil to me. You treated me like you hated me and now you're hugging me. I don't remember you *EVER* hugging or kissing me. However, I am very familiar with the back of your hand."

"Oh my God, Joan. My life was a living hell. Every time I met someone, I thought that he was the one. The one who was honest and caring. The moment I had sex, I got pregnant, and then I found out that he really wasn't the one. I was weak, uneducated, and they all thought that I was easy. I was looking for love from the men that came into my life. What I didn't know was that I couldn't recognize real love if it hit me in the face. After your youngest brother was born. I kept bleeding and the doctors thought that they were hormone problems and all kinds of other health issues surfaced. I couldn't keep regular visits to the doctor and I couldn't afford to take proper care of myself. I just couldn't. A few years went by and eventually I was diagnosed with cancer. I had five children and didn't know who would take care of them. I was told that I had an aggressive form of cancer and that it would take my life. The men in my life were trying to hump my thirteen-year-old daughter, Yes, I knew. Honey, you were young and beautiful and I couldn't protect you. I was angry. I was damn angry. I worked hard in a dry cleaners and I ran that place for a pittance.

Joan, I was battling cancer for ten years and raising five children. I was sick and tired and had no one. No one that I could turn to for help. I couldn't even take the chemotherapy. I couldn't burden you with four kids while I lay up in the bed sick from the side effects. I was depressed and I felt every negative emotion possible and it manifested in my attitude"

"Mama,"

"No Joan, let me finish. Our life stunk, I know. On the day that you left, I was on my way home to tell you that things were going to change. My employer, you remember Mr. Hawkins?" Mavis chuckled. "That black man was very rich and had no relatives. He died and left all of his money, and his three dry cleaners to me. He said that I knew the business and he felt safe leaving things in my hand. He was right I worked my hands to the bone for him. I moved from not even making it from paycheck to paycheck to a businesswoman.

Well, honey, I had some money and I had some hope and everything changed. I forgot all about my cancer. My big son," she smiled when she said the words. "Jonathan, you know he got that name by mistake, when the nurse brought him into me and I saw his nametag. I said, 'that's not what I named him' and she said, *'leave it. It means God's gift.'* Well let me tell you, your brother Jonathan and I worked so hard we opened thirty-four more stores and sent your other brothers to college and graduate school. Joan, my heart ached for you. I spent many sleepless nights wondering. Is she alive? Is she dead? My imagination worked overtime and I couldn't bear it. I saw you being abused, murdered, I thought of the worst things. I paced the floors many nights. In my quieter and saner moments, I wondered. *Did she make my mistakes?* And I prayed. 'Lord please take care of my little girl."

Joan's anger mounted. "Lord! Where was the Lord when I was growing up? I prayed all my life and he never answered.

Where was He when I ran away? Mama, I lived in Hell! Don't tell me about your "Lord" because clearly he didn't give a damn about me! I worked hard and made a better life for myself. I did it, Mama, not Him. He had nothing to do with it."

Mavis came close to Joan and she put her finger to Joan's lips. "Hush, baby. You don't know what you're saying. He was always there with you. I don't know why you ran away the very day He changed our lives, but He had a plan. I believe that. Had you stayed, would Megan be born? She is a beautiful child."

"But Mama, I made so many mistakes in my marriage and especially with Megan."

"Joan, I thought that every relationship I had was a mistake. I thought that every pregnancy was a mistake. Working all those years in a job that paid me next to nothing and Oh Lord!" The tears streamed down Mavis's cheeks. "The way I treated you came to my mind daily and that was my biggest mistake. Honey, I've lived a long time and I know that the Lord takes our mistakes and turns them into great big miracles.

We looked for you Joan, and we couldn't find you. Joan we tried. I stopped seeing the doctor. I accepted the Lord and joined the church and decided to live my life until the Lord took me. For me, time passed slowly and a few years ago, I found out that I never had cancer. It was good news. It gave me hope of seeing you again."

"Mama, I am so sorry about the cancer, I had no idea."

"How could you? I didn't tell you. I also didn't tell you that I love you. I prayed, my only desire was to see my only girl child once more before I died, and here you are.

Her mother held her off a little and looked into her brilliant black eyes and Mavis spoke to Joan's spirit. She said, "Joan, I love you." Mavis pulled Joan close and whispered in her ear. "I really do love you. You are my only daughter." She stood face to face now and Mavis pleaded with her. "Please forgive me for every harsh and hurtful thing that I have said or done to you. Come back into my life. I need you."

Joan cried, she hugged her mother and she bawled her eyes out, the words I love you, from her mother's lips was all the healing she needed. She smiled and thought to herself, *no matter how old we are, we all need our Mama's love.*

"And Joan, I never really hated it when you called me Mama. As a matter of fact, that was the one thing I missed after you left. Your daughter, Megan, that child is a wonderful human being. You did a wonderful job with her."

That compliment coming from her mother was priceless to Joan.

Mavis said, "Megan told me everything, your prejudice and hatred for your father and every black man who reminded you of him, and she told me about Tom." With great compassion in her eyes, Mavis said, "I have a gift for you."

Joan took the large manila envelope from her mother's hand.

"Open it." Joan opened it. A very distinguished looking white man was in the picture. A paper folded in half had his name, address, and phone number written on it. She looked up at her mother with a questioning look.

"That is your father." The shocked expression on Joan's face prompted her mother to go on. "My mother worked for his family when I was a young girl. He liked to tease and fool around with me, but I always knew to stay in my place. One day, things went too far and I was rude to him. He slapped me, and then he raped me, to show me who was the boss: and here you are. You hated a black image you conjured up of your father, not knowing that all along he was white."

Joan was stunned.

"If you want to get in touch with him the information is there, but I wouldn't recommend it. He knows that you are his. He came to see you when you were born. He warned me to stay away from him and his family. He will never acknowledge you and that is why I never told you who he was." Mavis held the two ends of the apron she wore and then she stood up. She watched a puzzled Joan trying to process what she was told. "Honey, life happens, it just does. Black or white, people are people. I'm going to join the others." Mavis chuckled, "I had to show that son-in-law of yours how we really cook soul food. He might be black but he has no idea what soul food is. While you all were at the courthouse he and I were cooking. Come join us. Let's go eat our first meal as a family."

Mavis left Joan sitting on the sofa with the picture of her father in her hand. Minutes later a dazed Joan walked into the dining room and Jackson walked up to her. He said, "Joan, or should I call you, mom?" There was no response so he continued. "Welcome to our home." The children ran to Joan and Jacob said, "Are you our new grandma?" Joan stooped down to hug him and with the warmest smile she said, "I sure am." She hugged the children and she winked an eye at Jackson and whispered, "Thank you, son."

They all sat down around Megan's formal dining table and fellowshipped. They talked and laughed and caught up on the past history of the family and the great strides in progress that they all made. Joan learned that her brothers were not only successful professionals but were married to successful professionals and their children were living productive lives as well. With tears in her eyes Joan said, "I am so happy to see that all of you are doing so well."

Mavis with the brightest and biggest smile surveyed her family around the great big dining table and she said, "Joan this is what answer to prayers look like. The Lord has truly answered my prayers and I can see that he answered yours, too. Praise His holy name."

Megan was happy to see the family had been reunited; and there was plenty of love to go around. All the love that Mavis and Joan were looking for was right here, right now.

Megan said, "Mama, I know that it irritates you when I call you, 'Mama' and that is one of the reasons I did it. From now on I'll call you whatever you want me to. What would you like me to call you?" Joan and Mavis looked at each other and burst out laughing and Joan said to her daughter, "Megan, call me Mama.

THE END

Coming Soon: The Surrogate

Paul and Kathy Goldstein are wealthy and powerful attorneys. Kathy is a beautiful 40 year old who is unscrupulous and walks a thin line along the limits of the law. Known as a barracuda among her colleagues for winning her cases at all cost.

Unable able to have children, she enlists the help of her friend to find a surrogate against the wishes of her husband. Tragic events forces Paul into situations he wants no part of and he angrily lashes out.

This is a novel of power, sex, jealousy, hatred, and love.

About the Author

Janis Beresford-McLennan resides in Maryland. She is a wife and the mother of three children.

Janis_beresfordmclennan@yahoo.com
http://outskirtspress.com/megan

Breinigsville, PA USA
05 January 2011
252719BV00002B/264/P